FOGBOUND FROM 5

Additional text and Edited
by
Peter Mark May

Front cover (c) Mark West & Neil Williams 2011
Cover design by Mark West & Neil Williams
Front cover image (c) Karla Baker 2007 - used with
permission, all rights reserved
Back cover image (detail) (c) Suhopese 2006 - used under
creative commons licence, all rights reserved

Hersham Horror Books
Logo by Daniel S Boucher

Copyright 2011(c)
Hersham Horror Books

Hersham Horror Books

ISBN: 978-1467953436

All rights belong to the original artists,
and writers for their contributed works.

All rights reserved. No part of this book may be reproduced, scanned or distributed in any form, including digital and electronic or mechanical, including photocopying, recording, or by any information storage and retrieval system, without the prior written consent of the Publisher, except for brief quotes for use in reviews.

This book is a work of fiction. Characters, names, places and incidents either are the product of the author's imagination or are used fictitiously, and any resemblance to any actual persons, living or dead, or undead, events, or locales is entirely coincidental

1st Edition

First published in 2011

CONTENTS

Foreword
5

ALISON LITTLEWOOD
The Quiet Coach
9

NEIL WILLIAMS
Fal Vale Junction
25

MARK WEST
Last Train Home
51

ADRIAN CHAMBERLIN
Kriegsmaterial
71

PETER MARK MAY
End of the Line
99

Biographies
131

Hersham Horror Books

Also from
Hersham Horror Books:

Alt-Dead

Foreword

From James Herbert's seminal book to John Carpenter's creepy film, from stories of mist by Stephen King to the pea-soupers in Sherlock Holmes's Olde London town, there is something quite unsettling about fog. It takes away the boundaries of our comfortable suburban streets, and can hide anything: from vengeful demons to the angel of death, from ravenous rats to sadistic serial killers...

Now add to that the most worrying form of late night transport, the train journey. In a car you could drive off and lock the doors; on a bus, the driver is never too far away. A train at night can be a lonely thing, a frightening way to travel; and whoever steps aboard is with you until the next stop, however far that may be...

Peter Mark May
Hersham
November 2011

Hersham Horror Books

FOGBOUND FROM 5

It was the very last train to pull out of Waterloo Station that night, leaving platform 5 so late that it was already fifteen minutes into the next morning.

It was the graveyard shift for the train crew and the last hope of getting home for the passengers.

As the train pulled to speed past the tribal graffiti daubing on every junction box, inch of fence or wall, the London weather decided to draw in on the train. A thick fog rolled up from the Thames to cover the next stop, Vauxhall Station, with its pressing dark and swirling oblivion.

Only a handful of passengers were travelling on the late night train and all they wanted was to get home without delays or mishap. Not all of them were aware of the wall of fog, as the train vanished into it. Booze, boredom or fatigue had taken some into a nodding half-sleep state, leaving their books, copies of the Metro and text messages from loved ones unread.

Five of the passengers would never experience a train journey like it again...

Hersham Horror Books

1

ALISON LITTLEWOOD

The Quiet Coach

Kev always took the quiet coach, if only to enjoy the contrast, to make his own light shine more brightly. He headed for it now, jumping low and smooth over the barriers so the ticket officers wouldn't notice. He ran down platform five and swung himself onto the train just as the door hissed closed behind him: perfect. He slung his hold-all - not that it held much - over his shoulder, grinned at the 'Quiet' sign, and began to whistle as he entered the carriage.

When he did, the whistle faded.

Kev liked the quiet coach. He especially liked the seats with a table in the middle; not because he needed a table, but because it meant he could pick someone to sit opposite, to see if they would look at him, see if they would react. He especially liked it when that person was a stuffy businessman in a suit, who'd raise their eyebrows when Kev put his feet up on the chair next to him. Or an old woman with silver hair and powdered cheeks. Or women with kids, who'd look shocked when Kev swore at his MP3 player or his phone. Yes, he liked them a lot.

Kev looked down the length of the coach now, its lights bright after the dark outside. He felt cheated. He'd known the carriage would be quiet, but - *this* quiet? All he saw was row after row of blue-patterned seats, and every single one of them was empty.

Then he heard a sound - almost a word, almost a sigh. A soft, formless sound - a white sound, Kev thought - but he smiled again, all the same, because there was someone in there with him after all. He could just see the top of their head, from their place in the centre seats. The table seats.

Kev made his way down the aisle, tapping the tops of the chairs as he went. He didn't look too closely at the other passenger, just slung his bag down into the aisle and his body into the opposite chair. Then he looked at her, grinning broadly. It was better this way: oh, so much better. An almost empty coach, and him picking the very table she had chosen - yes, definitely all the better for creeping her out.

But the woman didn't appear creeped out. She just looked at him, barely curious, no expression on her face at all. Kev didn't like that. He glared, his eyes wide open and cold, and at last she looked away.

Kev could see her properly then. It was no wonder he hadn't noticed her at first: she was slumped so low in her seat - no, in her *body* - she hardly seemed to be there at all. She wasn't much to look at, either: her face was pale and her hair mousy, grease-dark at the roots, and her eyes were as sunken as her cheeks. Kev felt a twinge of recognition - *one of us*, he thought - then it was gone.

The tannoy crackled and a tired voice began running through a list of destinations, hopeless dead-end places, each not much different from the last. Then the train started to move.

Kev sat back, stared at the sign on the window showing a mobile phone and a set of headphones with a red line through them, and took out his MP3 player. He slapped it onto the table, put in the earbuds, turned it on and stopped himself from flinching as music blared into his ears. He grinned at the woman once again, knowing how the sound would be projecting outwards too, tinny and irritating.

She didn't react, just turned to the window as the train pulled out of the station. Kev looked at her reflection, clear against the dark brick, trying to read her eyes. Then the image was gone, as the darkness was replaced by a dense pale fog that pressed itself against the glass. He pushed himself up straighter, staring out. There was nothing to see at all; only that blank white, blotting out the world.

A loud hiss intruded, replacing the music and the distant sound of the train, and Kev whipped the headphones from his ears. He could still hear that sound coming from them, nothing he could recognise; only noise, white noise. He flicked the player off. It was as if the fog had squeezed through the glass and entered the coach as sound.

He tried it again, skipping through the tracks, trying the radio; but there was nothing. His MP3 was fucked, just like everything else. He slammed his hand down on the table and swore. Saw that the woman was watching him.

She glanced at the window, looked back again. "Sorry," she said, as though apologising for the fog.

Kev scowled. She wasn't supposed to apologise. She was supposed to complain, make a fuss, look at him like he was dirt. That was what people did, and that was the way it was. She was supposed to shuffle uncomfortably, call him names; move to another seat.

"Where's your mum?" she asked.

Kev snorted. *Now*, he thought. *Here we go.* Though her voice had been nice; low and musical, gentle even.

"Is she waiting for you?" the woman said. Then she shrugged. "Probably not. It's just, it'd be nice if she was."

Kev started to fiddle with his phone. He could play a game on it, something with a loud, jangling soundtrack.

"Was it foggy, where you came from?" she sounded genuinely curious. Kev shot her a look. Would she never shut up? Now *she* was starting to irritate *him*. That wasn't the way this was supposed to go.

"Mind if we talk?" she asked.

This time Kev laughed, a sudden rough burst.

"Sorry," she said again. "I just thought—" another quick glance at the fog, then away. "I can't get away from it," she said. "It's always foggy, now. It'd be nice if - well, you know. If I talk to someone, it helps."

Kev was rapidly readjusting his opinion of the woman. She wasn't one of them, wasn't just some loser: she was obviously a complete nut-job. But she looked at him again, and her gaze was quiet, as though she was searching his face for something and actually thinking she might find it.

"My daughter died," she said, and Kev's lip curled. So that was it: she wanted some agony aunt to bleed over, and thought he was it. Well, he'd listen, but if she thought he could help - that was a joke.

"I had to drop out of school when I had Bethany," the woman began. "I resented her for that. Isn't that awful? There she was, my little angel, and sometimes I'd look at her and think about what I might be doing if she hadn't been born. If her dad hadn't taken off. It didn't mean I didn't love her, though; it didn't mean that. I think that was why I called her Bethany. It seemed a name that was fit for a little princess, you know? And she was. She was.

"Bethany was only four when she got sick. Cancer, gnawing away at her from the inside, like she was just something else to feed on. My little princess, she had golden hair when it started, all curly and long, not like mine. That went. She got all big-eyed, and her head was bald. I'd look at her sometimes and not know what had happened, like my little Bethany had been taken away and some little alien left in her place. And there were all those appointments, and the operations: they left big lines across her, like some toy had come unstitched and been sewn up again."

She stared out of the window, and Kev found himself looking for her reflection; it still wasn't there. Someone had taken the world and turned it white. No: grey - a damp, empty grey.

"My daughter used to say the fog was coming to get her," the woman said.

Kev started; looked back at her washed-out eyes.

"She got really bad, see. In the end they sent her home, said it was best for her, nothing they could do. So they sent this big bed for her to lie in, and all this - stuff, and drugs and things. And that was when I lost it.

"I couldn't cope, you see, not really. I was on my own, and it was all too much - and I got so I could barely look at her. I mean I loved her, loved who she was, but - it was like my Bethany was gone already, and I didn't recognise the one who was left. The one who cried till her face swelled up, who screamed at me, who hit me sometimes, when it hurt, you know? And I went off on one. I started drinking, did some harder stuff, injected a few times. It helped, but it didn't make it better, you know? Whenever I looked at her, my little girl, it just made it worse." She focused on Kev. "You ever injected?"

Normally he would have said yes, just to see what the reaction was. But he hadn't, not yet; though he'd wondered what it would be like to push a needle through his skin, into his veins, to find his blood. He shook his head, and she just nodded, like she already knew.

"I got so I didn't know what day it was, let alone when she was supposed to have this pill or that. I - ignored it, I think. Yes, I think that's what I was trying to do: ignore it. Only, when it reared its head, the sickness—" she paused.

"My daughter started to say there was a place called Emptiness, or The Emptiness, and that that's where she was going when she died. I thought it was just the cancer, making her say strange things. But these days . . ." she turned to stare at the whiteness, "I'm not so sure."

Kev followed her gaze and it was there, outside his window, formless and blank. He shook his head, looked back at the woman. And he waited.

"I never told her anything different, you see. I never told her she was going to heaven or to be a little star or a princess, none of that, not like I should have. I sometimes think that was how I let her down the most, you know? Not by ignoring her or giving her the wrong doses or not giving her anything at all, but by all those things I should have said and didn't.

"She got obsessed with it, you know?"

Kev didn't answer. He just looked at her face, and wondered how long it had taken for the cheeks to sink like that; for the unhealthy colour to seep through her skin. He was starting to feel he wasn't there any longer, that he'd vanished into his seat and the woman was talking to an empty place. An empty place she could try and fill; a quiet coach to receive her voice.

"Do you think it's true?" she asked.

"What?" His voice seemed too loud, too gruff.

"That it's full of ghosts." She nodded at the window. "She said that's what the fog was. That it was the bodies of ghosts, only pressed so tight together you couldn't see the joins. She said it was full of them, and their voices. Not really empty, at all."

Kev didn't say anything.

"She started to be scared of it, really scared, only I didn't do anything. I didn't tell her any of those nice things I should have. And then she'd ask me to hold her tight, and sometimes I did and sometimes I didn't. Because by then - I'd started to hate her a little bit too."

Kev nodded. He suddenly remembered his own mother, clear like a snapshot: the short skirt, the fishnet stockings, the sharp high heels.

"It didn't help that the fog seemed to come more and more, the sicker she got. I'd check on her and it would be there, outside her window, white as winter, blocking everything out. It didn't seem fair; she didn't have long left, but she couldn't see flowers or the sky or anything like that, only that fog. A whole mass of nothing, just like she said. And the worst part is, I started to think it might be true: that there's some big, white, empty place that people go when nobody wants them."

Kev started; sent the dead MP3 player skittering across the table. She caught it under her fingers and left them there.

"When that night came," she said, "the fog came too. It was so close, like it was trying to get inside. I had to draw the curtains to shut it out, she was that scared it had come for her. And then I went into the lounge and opened a bottle, and I shut the door so I wouldn't hear her. It wasn't just her crying: it was what she said.

"'The Emptiness is here, Mummy,' she'd say. 'I can hear the people in it. Don't you hear them?' And she told me what they sounded like, those voices. Cold and quiet and still, she said. Still and quiet and *cold*.

"I took her painkillers, did I tell you that?"

Kev shifted in his seat. He wanted to look away, but he could see from the corner of his eye that the window was waiting for him: the white window.

The woman sighed. "She said to me once, she said: 'I'll come and see you, Mummy,' and she meant it to be something nice, you know, like we'd have tea and cakes or something after it was all over, only somehow it didn't quite seem like that. And I just kept looking at her, trying not to let it show that I didn't want to see her, didn't want her clammy skin on me, didn't want that look in her eyes or her stinking sickbed smell."

She started to cry, silently, two smeary tears running down her cheeks.

"Do you think you'll have kids?" she asked suddenly.

Kev met her eye, startled. He shrugged. Shook his head.

"You should go home. Be with your mum."

That short skirt, those heels, the smeared red lips. Kev grimaced.

"Well, maybe not. But you should find someone. Care for them."

Kev met her gaze and squirmed under it. "I have someone," he said.

"Oh - that's nice. That's nice. You hang onto them."

Kev shifted. He couldn't seem to get comfortable. He listened for any other sound - the train rattling over points, rumbling through the night, but he couldn't seem to hear it. The fog seemed to stifle everything; everything except the woman's voice. He stirred. "She's called Gemma," he said.

And that was better, because now he could see Gemma's face, too: her healthy skin, cheeks that weren't hollow, hair that was chestnut-glossy, eyes that shone. *Shone.* That was what he'd first noticed about her, that made him know she was different.

The woman nodded as though he'd said everything out loud. "Don't let her go," she said again.

Kev didn't say anything. He just looked out of the window at the endless white and, for a moment, saw something else: a red speck in a red place, somewhere without shape or form.

"Where you going?" she asked.

After a moment, he answered. "To stay with mates. Gonna earn some money. Start something." His voice tailed away, swallowed by the fog. He couldn't get that thing he'd seen out of his head. He wondered if it could see him too, that speck, without eyes; if, somehow, it already knew about him.

"So you can marry her, is that it? You going to marry her?"

He shrugged.

"I'm not going anywhere," she said. "Just riding the trains. I thought I might be able to get away from it, this time. Keep ahead of it, you know? But nothing works."

"What?" Kev heard the contempt in his own voice, and the familiar sound of it made him feel a little better. "You what?"

"It comes with me, the fog. It won't ever leave me alone: not like I left her. It's like she said, she's come to visit. And she loves her mum, doesn't she." The woman paused. "Do you think that's true - do you think she still loves me, or do you think she hates me now? Now she knows everything, and can see everything . . . do you think she does, just a little bit?" She looked at Kev. "Would you?"

He shook his head, pressing back into his chair. He looked around at the empty carriage, thought for a moment of changing seats, getting away from her. But he knew there was nowhere to go, not really. It was as though there was nothing left of them but this train, this night, and they were nothing but people who'd got lost, so long ago it didn't even seem to matter why any more. He opened his mouth, but couldn't find an answer. And then her words struck him for the first time.

"You're not saying it follows you," he said. "You're not saying the fog follows you." He tried to laugh. For a moment he thought he could see that laughter, a pale mist emerging from his lips: he pressed them closed.

The woman nodded. "I don't suppose you'll believe me," she said. "No one does. But she's here, and she's never left me alone. I haven't seen sunshine since she died, and never seen rain either: not where I am. Do you understand? There's only ever the fog. It always follows, no matter how hard I try to outrun it. And lately - I hear it, too. I don't dare walk anywhere, not on my own, anyway. Having people round me . . . talking, like this . . . it blocks them out, you know?"

She leaned back in her chair, heaved a deep sigh. "That's not the worst thing, though. Know what the worst thing is?"

Kev shook his head.

"The worst thing, the one I get scared of more than anything else, is: what if I'm wrong? What if the fog is only fog, and there are no people in it, and no voices? What if she's just dead, and that's all, and she's really gone for good?"

Kev stared at her. It struck him that, despite her words, the woman was already in the place she spoke of; it had come to get her, she was in The Emptiness, and by seeing her and talking to her it meant he was inside it too. He turned and saw the fog, still close against the window, white and still. Still and quiet and cold.

"You look after her," the woman said. "Your Gemma."

Kev sat bolt-upright in his seat. He looked at the table, saw her hand lying over his MP3 player and he snatched it away, shoving it deep into his pocket. She didn't react, just moved her hand.

"Don't let anything happen to her."

Kev jumped up from his seat, staring at the woman.

"Sorry," she said, as though their conversation had just started again at the beginning, as though he'd just stepped onto the train. As if to underline the similarity the tannoy crackled and the announcer began to call the next station. Kev looked at the window and he couldn't see it, couldn't see anything out there at all; but he could feel that the train had begun to slow. He could get out, stop talking to this crazy, sad, empty woman: he could walk away. He peered into the fog.

Don't let anything happen to her.

Gemma, with her face pale and her cheeks sucked in and her legs spread: looking at him.

No. There was only the fog, pressing its face against the glass. Trying to get in. The Emptiness.

Kev tried not to think of that red speck. It wasn't red, anyway; there was no colour in it. It wasn't even there. It couldn't see him, couldn't think about him: it hadn't any eyes, hadn't any voice.

Was there whispering, under the sound of the train?

Kev tried to listen. There only a faint silvering sound, like the sound that had come over his headphones, but softer, quieter. It was the blood in his ears. The train, running over the tracks. He looked back at the woman and she was staring out of the window, her gaze distant, like she wasn't really seeing anything anymore, wasn't really thinking of anything now she wasn't talking to him.

It blocks it out.

The train began to slow and there came the bright squeal of brakes.

Soon he could walk away. He could go outside, to where his new life was waiting: away from this strange woman, away from everything he had known. Away from *her*. He shook his head, remembered the way Gemma had looked at him as the nurse placed the mask over her face; the expression in her eyes. The way the light in them went out.

It's for the best, Kev had said. *For both of us.*

And it had been better, afterwards, that he should leave: to let them both start something new. To start to forget, to blank it out, like some white, dank fog.

Kev turned his back on the woman, turned his back on the window. How could it have been different? He couldn't have saved it, couldn't have cared for it. He'd said he had friends waiting for him, a job, maybe, but he had lied. There was nothing. How could he have raised a child, saved it from the Emptiness, from the fog? He'd been living in it all his life.

He went to the door, saw again that damp whiteness. *What if I really hear it?* he thought. *What if I step out and I really can hear it, after all? What then?*

The train stopped and he stepped forward and pressed the button to open the door. It was the way it was, he told himself. Sometimes things happened because they happened, and nothing more. It was no use looking for reasons. The door slid open and he stepped out, breathing in the fog, taking it into himself. The air was cool around him. He told himself it was only fog; only that, and nothing more.

It was all right, standing in the fog. No one could see him and he couldn't see them. He couldn't hear anything either, not at first.

He didn't speed his steps and he didn't slow down as he walked away. The fog moved in close, like a caress. It lay against him and clung to him as he went, and the feel of it on his skin was like the gentle touch of a cold, cold hand.

Fogbound From Five

2

NEIL WILLIAMS

Fal Vale Junction

"It was always the same. I'm waiting on the station platform. But I don't want the train to come. A fog is rising, dense and sinuous. It's hard to make out, but a couple of hundred yards to my right is the mouth of the railway tunnel. I can't see the train yet but I can hear it rattling along the track. I imagine the other passengers waiting with me hear it too, but I don't turn towards them. There's something about them that frightens me as much as the approaching train. Nobody speaks and nobody moves; they just linger, grey shadows in the encroaching fog. I start to sense that they're not waiting for the train at all." Andrew Chambers paused, plucked the plastic lid from his coffee and tested the temperature.

"And then you wake up?" Andrew looked up to see Diane watching him intently, the hint of a question still on her lips; he always found it hard to hold her gaze, those cool blue-grey eyes seemed to pry into his innermost thoughts.

"Then...," he said, shaking his head, "the train arrives. At first I can see nothing, then the fog around the mouth of the tunnel starts to billow and I see a flash of light. The next thing I know the train comes thundering out of the dark, the illuminated coaches in tow cast a ribbon of light that rushes along the ground beside it. The light washes up the platform and envelopes me and I look up into the passing carriages where I can see the silhouettes of passengers. Then I notice that the ribbon of light is broken, one carriage towards the end of the train has no lights on. I turn to follow its path as it rushes by and I see the figure of a man pressed against the window. He appears to be shouting, or screaming."

"And then?"

"That's when I wake up," he said.

"The train never stops?"

He shook his head. "It doesn't even slow down."

"What about the other people waiting?"

"I can never bring myself to look back at them."

"And you can't even remember the name of the station. Perhaps it's a real place?"

Andrew shook his head. "I've seen that name countless times, but I can never remember it. I doubt it's real, but I do know where it is; or was, I should say."

"How can you know where something is and not know if it's real or not?"

He glanced down the bustling concourse of Waterloo Station to where the great clock was suspended beneath the vast patchwork of glass and metal. He could see from the greying light that it was starting to get dark. The clinging fog that had settled over the capital earlier showed no signs of lifting.

"You've got ages yet, the last time I looked it was still running half an hour late."

"I suppose this waiting is the worst bit," he said. "Once on board and away I'll be just fine."

"Like a dentist's waiting room," Diane said with a nod. He turned back to her, feeling glad she'd come to see him off.

He shook his head. "A fear of dentists is perfectly rational, they'll most likely cause you pain. I can even understand Arachnophobia, it's perfectly reasonable to be afraid of something that might do us harm. Like some form of race memory. But this is plain daft when you really think about it."

"You don't think your Sider - thingy - phobia is as serious as Arachnophobia? I'd say you're at greater risk from a train than a spider here."

"It's Siderodromophobia and thanks for that, you're a great comfort."

"I thought you said you were okay now?"

"That's what I'm here to find out; I haven't had any more dreams since the hypnotherapy sessions."

"If you'd mentioned this little adventure of yours earlier I would have offered to come along with you," she said, for once looking serious. "Keep you out of trouble."

"And what would Jerry say about that?"

"Well, when I left this morning I told him we were planning to elope."

"You're a bad, bad woman."

"I want to die. If only I could die..." She placed the back of a hand to her forehead and slumped rather melodramatically into her chair.

"Please don't you dare start with that *Brief Encounter* nonsense again," he said.

Diane had known Andrew for years. They first met when Andrew joined the company where she worked as a P.A. Initially she found him very aloof and not easy to approach. She even thought that he might be gay. It was only after several months working together that she finally understood what he was about. She'd learnt of the early tragedy in his life from office gossip, because Andrew never really talked about himself. They developed a good relationship as she found him less prickly and picked up on the more fragile, sensitive side to his nature. She imagined it was the mothering instinct in her – Diane and her husband were childless – and also Andrew's own desire for someone to fill that role. Although he had friends, even the occasional girlfriend, he was one of those people who seemed to drift through life without ever really connecting with it. Even as good friends he rarely spoke to her about his childhood; there was always a part of him that remained an enigma.

It seemed odd to Diane that it would be his phobia that would prompt him to finally open up to her, but it was an opportunity she wasn't going to allow to pass. "You were telling me about this station of yours."

"I was, but it wasn't my station, it belonged to my dad," he said and raised the cup to his mouth.

"Wait a minute. Your dad owned a railway station?"

"No, nothing like that, but you have to understand that this whole phobia thing is in some way connected to it and by something I found after Uncle George died. The dream was just the tip of the iceberg. I haven't even been on the tube since that time I flipped out. You know how bad that was."

"Lucky you weren't carrying a rucksack or they'd have probably shot you."

"Quite."

"But wouldn't it have been better to start with something less ambitious, like a short ride on the tube?"

"I really don't think I'm ready for that many dark tunnels on my first journey. And anyway, it's only a couple of hours to Yeovil. I know the route well enough so there'll be no nasty surprises." He caught the look on her face. "I know what you're thinking, but it's the journey not the destination I'm thinking about. My uncle's house was sold months ago."

"Then what about this mysterious thing you found?"

"Mysterious? I'd hardly call it that. Do you know what O Gauge is?"

"You mean toy train sets like Hornby, right?" She watched as he blew on the steaming cup.

"They're hardly toys and twice as big as the type you're thinking of. They're just double O," he said and put the coffee back down. He held both hands out to her in a typical fisherman's 'the one that got away' gesture. "With O Gauge the locomotive alone would be about this big."

She raised an eyebrow and gave a snort of laughter. "I see you know what really impresses a girl."

He could feel his cheeks flush and looked about the busy station. Nobody was paying them any attention. "Can't you keep a straight face for more than a minute?"

"I'm sorry, you just look so serious. I can't help it."

"It was last year, just after Uncle George's funeral. You probably remember I went back home to sort out his estate and clear the house, ready to put it on the market. I was sorting through some old boxes I'd found piled up under the stairs. There were old photographs, a few of Mum and Dad..."

He broke off to take another sip of his coffee.

"I was so young when they died, I don't really remember as much as I'd like. George and Sylvia never really dwelt on what happened; perhaps it was for my benefit. They were the ones left to bring me up after all. It must have been hard on my uncle to lose his brother like that. And then the business going under; Dad and Uncle George were partners, you know.

"Anyway, I was pulling these boxes out and right at the back I find another box. It was a dark blue, leather effect box with a hinged lid. Oblong, about..."

He was about to indicate the size with his hands again, but thought better of it.

"What it originally housed I have no idea. But inside, wrapped in old newspaper, was this model railway carriage. It was a rather drab looking, blue and grey British Rail Inter-City passenger coach. Several painted plastic figures were dotted around the interior, mostly business types in black suits and bowler hats. Towards the rear a guard was standing in the corridor, and beneath the peaked cap a rather crude attempt at a moustache was scrawled across an otherwise blank face. A moustache I'd drawn on myself.

"I recognised it as part of Dad's old model railway, but I couldn't account for how my uncle could have come by this when nothing else of my parents survived the fire."

"You survived," she said. Andrew was silent for a moment as if contemplating a suitable reply.

"For years, way before I was born, dad had been a model railway enthusiast. He set up a railway track in the garage, much to my mother's irritation and would spend most weekends adding to it. By the time I was six it filled the entire garage space. It occupied its own hand-built landscape of rolling hills, copses, little villages and a small country railway station just like the one I told you about." He stopped to let the final words sink in, and by the look on her face he knew they had. "Dad built everything. He even wired the whole thing up so every house and street would light up. Overhead, strings of Christmas tree lights would represent stars. Even the passenger coaches had little lights placed in them. He'd never let me play with them, of course. But he'd let me watch as the trains whizzed round the track. My favourite one wasn't a steam train. I hadn't a sense of nostalgia for a bygone age like Dad must have had. I liked the most modern looking ones, in this case a blue and grey Inter-City diesel locomotive.

"Before bedtime I remember how he would dim the lights and we would watch as the trains would travel through their own little night-time world. It was the most magical thing I remember about being with my dad. Then he used to send me off to bed warning me that if I stayed up too late a ghost train would come for any naughty boys not already tucked up.

"Of course what I wanted to see, more than anything, was a ghost train."

"And did you?" asked Diane.

"Did I what?"

"See a ghost train?"

"Of course I didn't. At least I don't think I did. It wasn't until I found the carriage that I gave any thought to what had happened. And then the dreams started and...," he paused as if trying to remember something. "It was the night my parents died," he began.

"I was a few weeks shy of my eighth birthday. Dad would never let me near the trains unsupervised, even during the school holidays when I had the best chance to get in undiscovered I always found the door to be locked. Dad knew me too well to trust me when he was out at work. My frustration at not being able to play with the railway during these otherwise empty days was more than I could take. I begged my dad but he always told me I was too young and couldn't be trusted to look after something that valuable. Months earlier he'd caught me drawing faces on a group of freshly painted commuters with a marker pen when his back had been turned, and since then my time spent there had been strictly limited to those few scant minutes each night.

"Every evening after I was bathed and ready for bed he would bring me down and together we would watch the trains. During the winter months when it would already be dark outside he would dim the lights, leaving only the constellations of false starlight sparkling overhead. This was my favourite time, watching the illuminated carriages snake around the track until the threat of the ghost train was invoked and it would be time for bed.

"Dad would carry me out, my head nestled against his shoulder. I would watch as he shut the door on the miniature world, but never once did I see him lock the door at night. Now I saw my chance to have the railway to myself and, just possibly, see this ghost train. But what time might such a train appear? If I was going to risk so much I wanted to be sure it would be worth the trouble I would be in if I was caught. I don't recall being particularly afraid, I felt only a frisson of excitement for what lay ahead. I was nearly eight and I think then I already suspected my father of making it up. There was no phantom train any more than there was a Father Christmas, but I was determined to find out for myself. Of course, quite what I would do with this information without giving myself away was something I never once considered.

"I set the alarm on a fold-away travel clock to just before twelve. Midnight was to be the chosen hour. I then placed the clock under my pillow so the sound of it ringing would not be heard by anyone other than me.

"All this went according to plan, and when midnight approached I crept on slippered feet downstairs. I didn't expect my parents to still be up, but a thin sliver of light beneath the door at the end of the hall confirmed I was not the only one still awake.

I considered there and then abandoning my plan, as from beyond the closed door I heard the sound of raised voices. It didn't sound like my parents' voices at all and I imagined it could only be something on the telly. It was much too late for visitors, though I do remember many occasions when my parents entertained until late into the night. I would sit at the top of the stairs listening to the rumble of voices and the clink of glasses to the accompaniment of a Johnny Mathis record. Johnny Mathis, now *that* would be a phobia I could live with.

"As I watched, the narrow slit of light darkened. Afraid of discovery, I ducked into the alcove that served as a cloakroom. This led to Dad's study and ultimately the garage. Here I waited for the door to open, pressing myself into the coats that hung along the wall. I breathed in the different heavy odours that clung to the thick material; the familiar smells of tobacco on Dad's old coat were strangely comforting. Though there was another scent I found within the folds of the coats that was less pleasant. I was relieved when the door did not open, and felt it was safe to move on.

"I was at the point of no return, going back risked greater chance of my discovery than if I were to carry on. I stepped out of the shelter of the coats and approached the door to the study.

"Not daring to turn on the light I navigated my way through the jumble of books and boxes using the edge of the desk as a guide. At the door that led to the garage I paused. Would it be locked? Had my understanding of Dad's habits been wrong? The thought suddenly occurred to me that the reason I never saw him lock the door was because he always intended to return there after I was soundly asleep. I imagined it was too late for him to have any further business in there that night, but in the hours since I had gone to bed he had doubtless been back to the garage. Even as I reached for the handle I felt I had been thwarted. I slowly turned the handle and pushed, fully expecting to meet with resistance. But the door swung easily inwards.

"From here I felt it would be safe to turn on the lights. The windows that might betray my presence were not visible from the house and only someone entering the study would suspect my presence. Any risk that the sound from the railway might be heard was minimal. I had ensured that both study and outer doors were firmly shut. The latter was heavy and well-insulated against the chilly interior of the garage.

"It was dark inside, and the windows in the external wall and main doors helped little. They were little more than insipid yellow rectangles of frosted glass illuminated by distant sodium streetlights. On tip-toe I fumbled for the light switch and found it almost immediately. I didn't turn this on but, satisfied it was the first in line, felt my way along until I located the switch that I wanted.

"Now with enough light to see by I was able to venture down the three concrete steps and locate the model's power supply. Beneath the faint glimmer of false starlight I set about bringing the villages and farmhouse that were dotted across the undulating landscape of papier maché and wood to life. As I pressed each plug firmly into the block of sockets, sections of the diorama would become illuminated as windows and streetlights flickered on. Finally, all that was left for me to do was to start the train.

"I had watched carefully how Dad set everything up; once everything was plugged in operating the trains would be easy. The train track consisted of two parallel sets of rails, which would allow two trains to run around the tracks counter to each other. Each track had its own control box with a central dial that when turned determined the speed of the train. I noted, with some disappointment, that there was only one train on the tracks. I hadn't spotted it at first as only the trailing carriage was visible from the mouth of a long tunnel that disappeared beneath a swathe of cattle-populated farmland. It was the same blue and grey liveried Inter-City diesel Dad and I had played with earlier that evening.

"I located the correct control box and slowly turned the dial. There came a slight humming sound and the carriages crawled into the tunnel. I followed the imagined course of the train to the exit on the other side of the hill. I could hear the rattle of the wheels on the tracks; it sounded much louder than I thought it would and I was suddenly afraid I might be discovered. I had no way of knowing how far the sound might travel into the rest of the house.

"It was by the station that the train came closest to the edge of the table. From this vantage point I could look directly into the dark, semi-circular mouth of the tunnel. The small figures on the platform remained impassive but I could feel my excitement rise as the train appeared from the tunnel with light spilling from the carriage windows. It seemed to come directly for me then, at the last minute, it veered to my left, following the curve of the track. So close it came to me I could feel the breeze from it on my face. The glow from the illuminated interiors washed across my face. At speed everything was a blur but if I blinked fast enough when each carriage shot by I could see clearly enough the bowler hatted figures seated within.

"The train was nearly passed me when the ribbon of light suddenly broke. I couldn't help but topple backwards as I was plunged into unexpected darkness. The final snapshots I had were of the interior of the darkened carriage and of a tiny, startled face looking out of one of the windows directly at me. By the time I'd righted myself the train was beyond my reach. I watched as it skirted round the far corner of the table; of the six carriages it pulled, one - the fifth in line - was in total darkness.

"I made no attempt to stop or reverse the train even though the control to do so still lay in my hand. I simply watched it course around the track. It didn't seem possible to have seen what I thought I had. My only explanation was that one of the plastic figures must have become unglued and fallen against a window. Anything more I had seen I put down to the lack of light, my own tired state and an increasing haze that seemed to fog my vision. It was only then, as I looked across the full expanse of the model, that I noticed how impaired my view of the railway had become.

"I was aware for the first time too of a cloying smell of wood smoke that had until that moment remained unnoticed over the pungent odour of solder that always inhabited the garage. A thick fog appeared to be rolling across the miniature world and I was aware that I could no longer see the brick walls beyond. The landscape before me was suddenly horribly real.

"I sensed the darkness extending over me and I looked up to see the stars eaten up by rolling clouds. I was frozen to the spot, lost and afraid. I could taste the acrid air on every breath I took, tears flooded my eyes and the fading streetlights of the distant villages rippled like mirages. I pressed my hands over my face, trying to shut out both the smoke and the sight before me. What I couldn't keep at bay was the relentless rattle of the wheels on the track. From the change of tone I knew that the train was approaching again and about to enter the tunnel.

"I peered through the cracks of my fingers and saw the train just before it slipped from view. It reminded me of a centipede scurrying for a fresh bolthole when the rock that shelters it is lifted away. I remained frozen to the spot, the clattering wheels sounding out the countdown to the train's reappearance. I focussed my attention on the tunnel exit and waited, crouched beneath the roiling clouds of smoke that now obscured the tangle of fairy lights. It was almost too dark to see, too dark to breath.

"At the same moment the train thundered into view, a light fell across the table as if the door to Dad's study had been opened. I could feel the heat on my back but I didn't turn around to look because the train was already upon me. The illuminated coaches rushed past, the passengers as impassive as before. But I was only interested in the darkened carriage and as it came through the station I saw a movement within.

"It's here that my memory of what happened seems to have become confused with that dream. What I think I saw can only be explained as part of the dream, because what I saw couldn't possibly have been real." He looked up at Diane as if he'd forgotten she was there, that he was really telling her the story.

"I saw a man, an actual living man at one of the carriage windows. I couldn't see his face clearly as everything was moving so fast and he was so small but he appeared to be shouting or screaming to me just like in the dream. I instinctively reached out and grasped the coach, pulling it towards me. At that very same instant an arm snaked about my waist and I was lifted up and carried to safety. I saw the remaining carriages buckle as the unbalanced locomotive took the corner and was derailed. My last memory was of the train tumbling from the table, trailing carriages and then smashing onto the cement floor."

After a long silence that suggested Andrew had no more to add, Diane asked, "Who carried you out?"

"A fireman, I guess; the house was fully ablaze by then. Not that I knew it at the time."

"You were lucky. If you'd have been in bed…"

"I would have died as well, I know that."

The public address system chimed and the two of them tilted their heads towards the sound, trying to pick out the words over the surrounding bustle.

"That's you then," said Diane as she stood up, leaving her coffee half-finished. "Come on, I'll wave you off."

"There really is no need, I'll be just fine." Andrew shouldered his travel bag and stumbled after her.

"I bet no one has ever waved you farewell from a station before."

"Well, no. Just promise me you won't do anything embarrassing, like run along the platform as the train moves off."

They moved smartly through the throng of passengers towards the platform, pausing only for a final check on the information board.

"One thing you never asked me," Andrew said.

"What's that?"

"About the fire, how it started."

"I guess I just assumed it was an accident," she said, finding a path through groups of bemused looking travellers that had congregated in front of the row of screens.

"Yes, I always thought so and I was always led to believe that by my uncle and aunt. But..." he sidestepped someone pushing a trolley. "When I found the model carriage at my uncle's, I noticed an article in one of the newspapers it had been wrapped in. It said there was evidence that fires had been started throughout the house. It wasn't an accident."

"Christ, that's terrible." Diane stopped and turned to face him. "You mean someone..."

He shook his head. "No, no one else was suspected. How do they always phrase it in the news reports? 'The police are not looking for anyone else in connection with this incident.'"

Diane reached out a hand to him. "I'm so sorry," she said.

"I can't really understand why Dad would do such a thing. Now, with Uncle George gone, I haven't a hope of even getting close to understanding what was happening back then. Even with all the problems with the business, what would have driven him to do such a thing to Mum - and to me? Dad had all manner of solvents and such like in the garage so he certainly had the means to hand. I even remember the smell of something like paraffin from one of the coats as I hid outside the study door.

"I suppose that's what the dream was all about. The man at the carriage window has to be my father, don't you think? I mean, who else could it be?" Diane knew he wasn't expecting to get any answers from her. "And what is he trying to tell me? That he's sorry for killing my mother, himself; destroying the life of blameless child. I want to hate him, but for some reason I just can't bring myself to do it."

"I really think you should postpone your trip."

"No, I need to do this more than ever," he replied. "I'm fine, really I am."

"You're sure about this?" she asked, her eyes searching into his so intently that he had to look away.

"Yes, I'm sure."

There was something in his tone of voice that informed Diane he was resolute. "Well, come on then, you don't want to miss it."

They walked down the platform, Diane holding his arm. "Last chance to back out," she said and noted the shake of his head and decided not to ask again. "Which carriage is it?"

"Coach E, this one I think?" he checked it against his ticket.

"I think the fog might be lifting but it's so difficult to say for sure," she said, peering along the platform into the fading daylight.

"Well, a train leaving on a foggy night, it's such a cliché. It's your dream come true. No wonder you wanted to wave me off."

"Piss off!"

"Ha! I bet you wouldn't catch Celia Johnson using language like that."

"All right Trevor Howard, what have you got to say?"

"We'll always have Paris?"

"Don't be daft, that was Bogart in *Casablanca*."

He made as if he was about to step onto the carriage then turned. "I think I remember the name of the station; it just came to me then," he said.

"The one from your dream?"

"And the model railway, it's something like Fall Vale Station."

"Junction? Fal Vale Junction?"

"Yes, that's it! How could you know? You've heard of it before then, it is real?"

"No - at least I don't think so. It's from a film."

"Not *Brief Encounter*, please?"

"No, not that," she paused as if reluctant to continue. "It was called *The Ghost Train*."

It was only as he watched the platform slide away that he realised he'd managed to board the carriage without once experiencing the feelings of fear or anxiety he imagined he would. He only felt a twinge of regret as he gave a final wave to Diane and watched her drift from view as the train eased slowly out into the veil of fog. The effect was strangely disconcerting, as if it were only the train that remained still and everything else was rolling backwards. It felt like a facsimile of reality, a backdrop painted with broad strokes on canvas then unravelled behind the static tableaux to give it the illusion of forward momentum. Like a scene from one of Diane's beloved films.

He watched the passing landscape shift from the grey oppressiveness of the city into night-blackened emptiness. Occasionally the fog would part to reveal the suburban sprawl of industrial estates, out of town supermarkets and cinemas, shining like beacons over the bejewelled car parks. By the time he'd reached open country it was too dark to see beyond his own reflection. Opposite him a young girl with a permanently furrowed brow tapped at her mobile phone. Occasionally a small boy would peep through a gap between the seats, obviously trying to read what she was texting. Above the steady clatter of the wheels and murmur of his fellow travellers he could hear the boy saying to the parent next to him, "What does Wer Ter Fer mean, that's not a real word, is it Daddy?"

Andrew smiled as the father shushed the child. He let his head fall back; he closed his eyes, the gentle undulating motion of the train slowly working its magic. Before sleep finally claimed him, he thought: *there's nothing to be afraid of*. It sounded loud in his head and he wondered if he'd actually spoken it. From beneath heavy eyelids he looked for a reaction from the girl with the phone. Finding none, he drifted into sleep.

It was the smell of something burning that first roused him. Not the unpleasant odour of burnt grease that he had encountered when climbing onboard. This was something more delicate: it brought forth memories of autumnal walks, Bonfire Night and...

He was immediately aware that something had changed. The carriage rattled along the tracks, the sound louder than that which had lulled him into sleep. That gentle rock was now replaced by bone jarring tremors; both legs felt numb and the seat beneath was hard to the touch and completely unyielding. His eyes snapped open and he found himself staring into unexpected darkness.

Why are there no lights? The girl with the phone was gone, as was the chatter of his fellow travellers. He squinted down the aisle; at various intervals he could see the occasional jutting shoulder that indicated some of the other seats were still occupied. He glanced at his watch, trying to ascertain the length of time he'd slept, but his fogged mind could make no sense of the pale luminescent numerals. He turned to the window and saw only the ghostlike reflection of his own face and the dark grey walls beyond. *A tunnel, I'm in a tunnel,* he thought, *but where, exactly?* The answer came almost immediately, as outside the walls to the tunnel were suddenly drawn back like a safety curtain to reveal a blur of foliage and beyond it a mist wreathed country lane that ran parallel to the rails. He pressed his face against the window, trying to see what lay ahead. He could see the sidings start to widen and the ground beside him rise, several hundred yards further on there was a light. Andrew could see it was a station. The train showed no signs of stopping here, but if he could at the very least identify where he was. As his carriage came alongside the platform he whipped his head back, trying to catch the name on the sign. None of the huddled figures that occupied the platform turned to watch as the train roared past. Every one of them remained fixed on the direction from which he'd come, lifeless as showroom dummies. Andrew backed away from the window, holding firmly onto the table to prevent himself being thrown across the carriage. Silently mouthing the fragments of the words he'd glimpsed on the sign, desperately trying to bring some sense of order to things.

He located the nearest passenger a few seats in front of his and called out to him.

"Excuse me," he said, carefully shuffling from row to row. Getting no response he moved yet closer; he could see a hand resting on the arm rest. Was he asleep?

He reached out to the exposed skin, touched it gently and instantly recoiled. Instead of finding warm flesh his fingers met with the same hard material as the seats. He pulled himself round the headrest to see for the first time the bowler hat and beneath it the blank face of a suited figurine.

Andrew staggered backward, losing a handhold on the back of the seat. The violent rocking of the carriage sent him sprawling on the floor. He righted himself as best he could and crawled on all fours towards the rear of the coach. He cast frantic glances left and right, looking for the communication handle, but the interior of the carriage proved as featureless as his fellow passengers face. He was a little way past his own seat when he was brought up sharply. His hand had fallen on a hard, smooth object on the floor in front of him. It was a shiny black boot.

He looked up at the conductor standing over him and started to whimper. One hand was tucked away from view as if reaching into a waistcoat pocket, the other held out with the palm exposed, as if frozen in the act of guiding someone to their seat. The face might have been as featureless as that on the seated figure but for a crude attempt at a moustache that in the constant shifting shadows looked more like a gaping downturned mouth caught uttering a terrible scream. But the only scream came from Andrew. Even without the figure that blocked his path he knew there could be no escape. That he had to see the journey through to its end. Sobbing, he pulled himself upright and looked down the length of the carriage, seeing for the first time the black domed hats of all the passengers that shared the coach.

He returned to his seat and looked out through the haze. He could see gentle sloping fields dotted with toy plastic sheep. There were men fishing by painted rivers and a small boy in shorts who always waved, whether there was a train there or not. In the valleys and from the hillsides picturesque villages and farmhouses glowed invitingly with light from five watt bulbs.

He looked up to see the churning smoke overhead. Were it not for burning that raged in his eyes and throat he might have still believed it to be clouds. Then he was plunged back into darkness as the train re-entered the tunnel. He closed his eyes against the stinging smoke and pressed his forehead hard against the clear plastic of the window and waited for the change in tone that would inform him the train had left the confines on the tunnel.

His eyes snapped open just as the train emerged and he saw the faux Victorian brickwork of the tunnel mouth. At that very same moment there came a bright light, searing its way through the choking haze. It looked like a far off column of yellow fire and was accompanied by a rush of heat that could be felt in the carriage.

As the train rushed through the station, past the waiting faceless figures, past the signs that read Fal Vale Junction, Andrew started to scream. But it wasn't at the sight of the boy staring down at him with bewildered, terrified eyes, he'd been expecting that.

It was the dark shape behind the boy that came shambling out of the column of smoke and flame. The boy reached out towards Andrew, clumsily snatching at the carriage, causing the train to buckle and jump from the tracks. It was at this moment that the figure, obviously insensible with drink, stumbled into plain view. Andrew could see the slackened mouth moving as if attempting to form words. The man's eyes bulged from a glistening mask of sweat, as if he were suddenly gripped by some madness, utterly unable to comprehend the scene playing out before him.

The very last thing Andrew saw before the train plummeted from the tracks and the screams of protesting metal drowned out that of his own was the sight of Uncle George gathering up the dumbstruck child.

Fogbound From Five

3

MARK WEST

Last Train Home

A taxi pulled up sharply outside the Victory Arch entrance to Waterloo Station and a cyclist went by, shouting obscenities. The driver didn't acknowledge them, but turned in his seat to look through the plastic panel.

"A tenner, mate."

Alex Griffin already had his wallet in his hand, not wanting to delay getting into the station and onto the train any longer than was absolutely necessary. He passed the note through the gap in the panel to the cabbie who took it, looked at Alex for a moment, then turned around with a sigh.

The taxi lurched back into the traffic as soon as Alex had slammed the door closed. He looked up at the architecture of the Arch and wondered if he loved this station because of its beauty and history or because it represented the last place he saw in London before heading home to his family.

A fog had descended on the city and wiped away from sight all existence of the stars, though the pale disk of the moon was just barely visible. Across the street, gaudy lights were becoming more ethereal by the moment and cars seemed to appear from the gloom without notice.

He checked his watch - the time was 11.52- and started up the wide stone steps into the station, taking out his mobile phone as he walked. There were no new messages. He pressed the key for his voicemail and smiled as he listened to the message his six-year-old son Sefton had left.

"G'night Daddy, sleep tight. See you in the morning." There was the sound of movement, then his wife said, "Okay, you can watch *Bullseye* now. Sorry Alex, that's as good as you're going to get. Safe journey, see you tonight. Love you."

He locked the keypad and slid the phone into his pocket. Just hearing their voices - Sefton fulfilling his duties and wanting to get back to what he was doing and Cathy holding the fort - was enough to keep him going. He hated to be away from them, hated being in London and he especially hated having to catch the last train home on a Friday night.

There were still plenty of people on the concourse, but he could move freely amongst them, as most were locked into their own little worlds - on the phone, on the Net, listening to music. He always took a little amount of satisfaction with this kind of human contact: it never asked for anything but it was nice to see other people desperate to leave the city and get home too. He stopped under the clock, looking up at the metal and glass grill of the roof but the foggy night just made it a mirror, showing him, looking at himself.

Alex put his laptop bag between his feet and shrugged his rucksack off. He wanted to take off his suit coat, but settled for taking off his tie instead and stretched, leaning to one side and rubbing the small of his back. Between sitting in meetings all day, the weight of his rucksack and general tiredness, he felt rotten. He decided that tomorrow he'd sleep in as long as Sefton would let him, then take the boy swimming. It'd do them both the world of good.

Alex looked up at the departures board; he already knew the platform and the time of the train, but it always paid to make sure. He heard footsteps and turned, ever so slightly, to watch a pretty blonde woman who looked to be in her mid-twenties coming towards him. She was concentrating on her smartphone. Her fine hair was in a pony tail and she wore faded blue jeans, sandals and a pale blue gypsy shirt. At the last moment, she looked up and saw Alex and side-stepped to avoid walking into him.

He smiled at her and she favoured him with one of her own. She had a warm, long face and the smile lit it up, sparkling her eyes. "Sorry," she mouthed.

"No problem," Alex said.

The woman stopped a few yards in front of him, checked the board long enough to get her bearings, then turned left and started to walk, the soles of her sandals making soft slaps on the tiled floor.

"Platform Five," he said softly and pulled his rucksack back on, grimacing as it pressed his damp shirt against his skin. As soon as he got on the train, he'd take his suit coat off and that couldn't come quick enough. He picked up his laptop bag and, aware that somebody was standing very close to him, turned.

A man was right behind him. He wore brown combat trousers, a T-shirt that was old enough for the transfer on it to be indecipherable and a black bomber jacket. He looked to be in his early thirties, a few years younger than Alex, with a thick mop of dirty blond hair.

"Hey," said the man and Alex felt ill at ease. It took him a moment or two to put his finger on it until he realised that the man looked almost feral. His eyes were small and dark, whilst his mouth and nostrils were wide. A junkie, perhaps, looking for a fix? A drunk, wanting another can of White Lightning to get him through the night?

"Yeah?"

The man smiled, baring his teeth and Alex was surprised to see that they were very white. "You couldn't lend us a couple of quid, could you? Been caught short, credit on my phone's run down and these bastard pay phones are like highway robbery."

"For the phone?"

"Yeah, mate, I need to ring me partner. Her and the kids, they'll be wondering where I am." The man shifted from foot to foot and twitched his nose, the movement pulling his top lip down over his teeth. "Didn't realise the credit was down." As if to prove his point, the man took a mobile phone out of his pocket, waving around like someone masquerading as a policeman in a cheap film. "You have to put a quid in to make the damned things work."

Alex looked around and saw no-one close to them. The blonde woman was away into the distance, heading for her platform. "Okay then, a couple of quid."

The man smiled again and Alex noticed something in the side of his mouth, something red and almost raw looking and then it was gone. "Cheers, mate." He held out his hand and nodded his head. "My name's Johnny, how do you do?"

"Alex," he said automatically and shook Johnny's proffered hand. He pulled change from his pocket, sorted out two pound coins and handed them over.

"Thanks Alex," said Johnny, "you're a lifesaver," and he walked off towards the bank of payphones. With that sinking feeling that he'd somehow been fleeced, Alex began walking in the opposite direction, towards Platform Five. After a few paces, he stopped and turned. Johnny was standing by the payphones so maybe he'd been on the level after all. Johnny saw him and raised a hand. Alex waved back. The man was still twitching his nose.

There weren't many other passengers for the last train, with perhaps only a dozen people on the platform. Most of them were business-suited men stood at the far end, their too-loud voices betraying a stop in the pub on the way home. A couple in their early twenties were sitting on a bench, him reading a paper, her resting her head against his shoulders. The man moved slightly and the woman's head tipped forward. She was asleep. Leaning against a support was the blonde, still checking the screen of her smartphone as if worried that she might be missing something.

The train was one of the Turbostar engines that he hated. They had no heft, but felt like tube trains that had grown a bit too much to fit into the underground network. There were two carriages sandwiched between the engines, so Alex was glad there weren't too many people waiting. Having to stand all the way home wouldn't make him happy.

The engine was idling, the driver talking to the platform guard. The driver laughed at something, nodded and got into his cab. A whistle blew and the business-men took their cue immediately, racing each other to get into the first carriage, laughing and giggling as they bumped into one another. The young couple on the bench got up, the woman yawning and rubbing her face. The blonde looked up and around, saw Alex and smiled, then got onto the second carriage.

Alex followed her on, passed the toilets and waited for the door to *shush* open. Through the glass he could see the couple at the far end of the carriage, huddled back in the same position they'd had on the bench, except this time the man was looking out of the window. The blonde woman was sat halfway up the carriage, facing the front of the train. Alex picked a chair two rows down from the door, put his rucksack and briefcase on the spare seat, took his suit coat off and folded it carefully. He put it on top of the rucksack and sat beside the window, pulling his MP3 player from the rucksack's front pocket. He put the headphones in and switched the player on, decided against getting his paperback out and looked out of the window as the train slowly rumbled out of the station and into the foggy greyness.

By the time the train was passing the Lambeth Road, Alex had started to doze and as they rattled through Vauxhall, he was asleep.

Alex awoke with a start and couldn't work out where he was or why he could hear Warren Zevon singing. He was slumped sideways, his neck stiff. He rubbed his eyes as he looked around and got his bearings. He was on a train and his MP3 player was still running.
Of course.
Something hit the side of the train hard, rattling the window his left arm was resting against. He sat up, wincing as his neck muscles slowly eased themselves into operation.
There was another thud, equally loud, equally hard. How could something be hitting the side of a moving train that hard? What was going on, were they being attacked somehow?
That thought made him smile in spite of himself - what a stupid idea. He sat up straight, rubbing his neck and looked out of the window. The combination of the darkness, the fog and the interior lights meant that he couldn't see anything other than a reflection of himself and the carriage. He paused the MP3 player and in the silence realised he couldn't hear the engine. That realisation bled into the next one - he couldn't feel any movement.
The train had stopped. Were they at the station already? He checked his watch, it was 12.45. Still a while to go yet. So had there been an accident, or was there a blockage on the line?

The thud again, harder this time and accompanied by a damp sound.

Alex slid across the empty seat and stood up in the corridor. He couldn't see the blonde woman but supposed she might have drifted off to sleep as well, slipping down her chair out of sight.

He turned towards the cab and could see that the driver's door was closed. Should he go and knock on it? Would that help anyone? If the train had stopped for a reason, he didn't want to be the pain-in-the-arse passenger who made life difficult for people trying to resolve the problem. He walked up the corridor, pressed the button and the doors shushed open. There was no-one in the gangway and nothing to be seen through the windows in the doors. Stepping close to the right hand side one, he leaned his forehead against the glass. It was cold to his skin. He could see himself, the mist outside making him look like a ghost.

Something moved in the murk, a quick shape that disturbed the swirls of fog but wasn't close enough for him to make out clearly. The driver maybe, checking something on the track? Alex shrugged - best not to get in the way - and started back for his seat.

At the end of the carriage, only the male of the young lovers was in his seat. He was slumped against the window with a red smear across his cheek that seemed to run into his equally red T-shirt.

As Alex sat down, the right earphone dropped onto his chest. He took the left one off, wrapped them around the body of his MP3 player and put it away in the side pocket on his rucksack.

Something hit the side of the train again, further down the carriage and a startled Alex heard something grunt. He looked up in time to see a face slide down the glass, pressed so hard against it that the left side was smooth and blank, a red-smeared sheet of paper. The one visible eye roved wildly and blood seeped from the mouth.

"Holy shit," said Alex, getting out of his seat quickly. Whatever was out there, he didn't want to be sitting near the window. "Holy shit."

The lover was still leaning against the window. "Hello?" Alex called. "Excuse me?"

There was no response, apart from a lighter thud against the side of the train. What the fuck was going on, was this some kind of nightmare that he'd woken up from, sweaty and scared, as the train pulled into the station?

"Hey," Alex called again to the lover, "hey, did you see that?"

The man didn't move and it took six strides for Alex to reach him. With each one, it became clearer what the smear was and that the T-shirt hadn't started out red.

Alex stood over the seats, in front of the door that led into the next carriage. It was dark beyond the glass and he couldn't see or hear anyone in there. Where were the businessmen? Had they got off, was that one of their faces he'd seen pressed into the window? He looked up and saw the toilet light was showing as vacant, so where was the female lover?

"Mate," he said, leaning over the chair, "are you alright?" But it was obvious he wasn't, that the man wouldn't - couldn't - answer. The smear on his cheek was blood, oozing from deep cuts that might have been slash marks but looked more like the result of a clawing. His neck was equally devastated, with gashes wide enough to show that he must have bled to death.

Alex stepped back, his heart beating like a techno track. He groped behind him for the seat headrests, trying to stay on his feet. His breath came in short gasps and he dared not close his eyes, in case the image of the carnage was imprinted on them forever. Whatever was happening, whatever had ripped this man's neck out, was still here. He staggered back a step, almost stumbled, grabbed a chair back. Something cool and soft touched his left hand. With a cry, he whirled around, fist ready and saw the blonde looking at him.

"What's going on?" she said, her voice lightly blurred with sleep. "What're you doing?"

She sounded so calm, so composed that he doubted himself for a moment. "Stay in your seat," he said, his voice harsh.

"Eh? What do you mean?"

Alex looked around, checking that the three of them were still alone in the carriage, then leaned over the seat back. "What's your name?"

"My name? What? You're scaring me, what's going on?"

"Tell me," he said, "what's your name?"

"Jenny, it's Jenny, what's happening?"

"Okay Jenny, I'm Alex and I don't know what's happening except that it's something bad."

Jenny put a hand to her throat. "What do you mean?"

Alex pointed at the smear of blood on the window. "That. And the man at the end of the carriage there."

Jenny made to stand up and he put his hand on her shoulder. "Don't."

"What's wrong with him?"

Alex checked the carriage again: still no-one else was around. The inter-carriage door was closed and still dark. "I think he's dead."

"Dead?" Jenny's eyes were wide. "Dead? Did you kill him?"

"What? No, of course I didn't kill him, I just woke up and there he was."

"Who did it then, his girlfriend?"

"I don't know, but we need to ring the police."

Jenny looked out of the window. "So where are we?"

A good question and one he hadn't considered. Where were they? How could he report a fatal incident when he had absolutely no idea where they were? He knew the line, he knew the route, he could tell them that they'd been travelling for less than forty minutes - but then, what if they'd been stopped for half that time?

The inter-carriage door *shush*ed open and Jenny grabbed his knee. Biting his lip, Alex turned slowly, not sure what to expect. It was the woman, the lover of the dead man and she was coming through the doorway on her hands and knees. Her dark hair was mussed and her hands and fingers were dirty. There was something hanging under her belly, dragging along the floor.

"Shit," said Alex. He couldn't see anyone in the corridor behind her and so started to move forward. Jenny grabbed his arm and he looked at her, her eyes wide. She mouthed *no* and he shook his head, turned back. The woman was still coming, slowly. He rushed down and knelt in front of her, his hands on her shoulders.

"Hey," he said quietly, "it's okay." The woman shook her still-hanging head twice. "Don't worry, we won't hurt you."

The woman shook her head again and collapsed onto her side. After a gasping breath, she rolled onto her back. Her eyes were closed and there were streaks of dirt and blood across her face. Alex leaned back and looked at her quickly, trying to gauge any major wounds but her neck and chest area looked clear. She moved slightly, with a jerk and he looked towards the door. A deep gash on her stomach had split open her T-shirt and her intestines were coiling out of the gaping wound. The glistening links led back through the doorway, where they were pulled taut. The woman moved again and groaned.

"What...?" he said and instinctively grabbed her under the arms. Her intestines pulled taut, then more lengths slid out of her stomach and she groaned again. Was he doing this, by pulling her back? If her intestines were the rope in this tug of war, any pressure would surely only make things worse.

Alex let go of her and her eyes opened briefly as she reached for his right arm. Her fingers closed over his cuff but couldn't gain purchase and slid off. She hitched back a few inches and then the door closed, trapping the string of intestine and making her grunt.

Something moved against the glass and even though Alex was staring at it, he couldn't take it in. How had this huge dog got on the train? How was it standing up? It took him a moment or two to realise that the huge shaggy creature he was looking at was dressed in the tattered remnants of Johnny's clothes from Waterloo. The combat trousers were now ripped and ragged and the bomber jacket was straining at the seams, but it was definitely him.

"Alex?" Jenny's voice was low and pitiful.

"Stay there, Jenny," he urged, pushing himself back along the corridor. The creature seemed to be lost in figuring out why yanking on the intestine wasn't bringing its prize closer, to busy with the puzzle to notice Alex.

"Sorry," he hissed at the woman, but she didn't reach for him this time and he could only hope that she was already dead.

Alex had worked his way back past four or five seats before the creature saw him. With an ear-shattering roar, it bashed on the door without pressing the release button. Alex watched the laminated glass curve under the onslaught. He heard Jenny scream behind him.

"Move to the end," he shouted, "get to the back of the train."

The creature roared again, pounding against the door with giant, hairy hands. Surely, however tough that safety glass was, it couldn't put up with much more abuse. The creature leaned its head down, breath clouds flowering on the glass from the large nostrils. The teeth, so many sharp, sharp teeth, glistened red.

Alex took a chance, turned and got to his feet. Jenny was edging backwards down the corridor, holding onto each headrest she passed, her eyes fixed on the monster from a hundred celluloid nightmares that was trying to get to them.

"How…?" was all she managed to say.

"I don't know," said Alex, "but keep going."

He grabbed her arm and pushed her towards the door. The wolfman continued to pound the glass behind them, roaring at the same time, creating a cacophony that filled the carriage and made Alex's ears ring. Jenny pressed the button for the doors and stumbled through. She managed to regain her balance and staggered to the exit door. She sprawled against it, her head bouncing off the window and she sat still for a moment.

"Jenny! Jenny!"

She shook her head and pushed up slowly.

Alex saw the safety hammer beside the door. He elbowed out the break-glass and pulled the hammer away from the catch that held it in place. The tool was lightweight, a thin pistol grip with a right angle of hard plastic at the end, tipped with a small metal ball. He'd been hoping for something heavier and more substantial but couldn't complain.

"Door's open, Alex, come on."

The howls stopped and Alex leaned back. The wolfman was gone. He turned as Jenny stepped out into the fog. She looked back at him, waiting. The fog had brought visibility down to a mere few feet and he couldn't see beyond the gravel that the train tracks rested on. Jenny stepped away from the train.

"Stand here," he said, "I can't remember which side has the other line."

"Shit," she said and jumped back beside the carriage. "What was that thing in there?"

How could he tell her it was a wolfman? That the bloke he thought was a junkie, who'd asked him for money to ring his wife and kids had turned into a monster that was probably even now feeding off the intestines of some unfortunate woman? "I don't know," he said.

"What was he doing to that poor woman?"

Again, what could he say? "I think..." he started and then Jenny was wrenched backwards, the wolfman's huge paws on her shoulders, the claws digging through her shirt. Blooms of blood appeared on the material. Alex saw a quick flash of the glistening snout and then he was on his own in the fog again.

He heard Jenny scream and the wolf howl and there was the sound of material ripping. Alex gripped the hammer and started to walk down the line, his right hand against the carriage walls. After a few steps, all he could hear was the crunch of gravel under his feet and the rapid pounding of his heart in his ears. There was no other sound. He began to move slower - what if the wolfman was waiting for him, taking advantage of the fog blanket? What if he walked directly into it?

Another step, another crunch. Something up ahead made a *snick*ing sound. His pulse seemed to get louder. Alex raised the safety hammer. Nothing moved. Eddies of fog swirled around him. He shifted on the gravel, the rasp of it far too loud. Nothing else made a sound.

Alex took another step and heard the rasp of breath the moment before the wolfman loomed in front of him, standing up on its hind legs, its wide maw open, the vicious teeth coated with blood and saliva. The stench was incredible and Alex stumbled back as the wolfman snapped its jaws where his face had been only moments before.

Alex was sprayed with saliva and blood but he regained his balance and brought the safety hammer down as hard as he could. The wolfman tried to move backwards and looked up, its lips curling. It wasn't fast enough and the tip of the hammer went into its left eye.

It howled in pain and pulled back. Adrenaline surging through him, Alex wrenched the hammer back; it finally came free with a wet, sludgy sound and he drove it back down. It caught the wolfman on the end of its snout, making it howl again. Alex raised it once more, leaning forward and aimed for the right eye but missed, smashing instead against the brow.

The wolfman's howl was so high pitched it almost became a scream. The beast pushed away from Alex, disappearing into the fog. Alex leaned against the carriage, trying to catch his breath. The adrenaline rush over, the shock of what had happened hit him all at once and he was sick. His arms began to spasm and he dropped the bloodied hammer.

He leaned forward, spitting the remaining bile between his feet. His breath came in ragged gasps and he stood upright, hands on his hips, taking as deep a breath as he could. The cool air felt good.

Gravel crunched and Alex felt a prickly coolness run up his back. The hairs on his arms and the back of his neck stood on end. Where was the hammer? He looked down, couldn't see it the ground clearly enough.

Another step on the gravel. "Alex?"

"Jenny, where are you?"

She stepped out of the fog, the front of her shirt wet and dark with blood. Her face was pale and there was livid blood on her neck.

"What did it do to you?"

"It bit me," she said and sobbed, "it bit me."

"Fuck. We have to get you sorted out. Come on, we'll get inside the carriage and get help."

"Why did it do that, Alex?" she said and fell against him. He grabbed her, trying to keep them both upright and then he heard the rasp of the wolfman. It seemed to be coming from behind him. He turned and there it was, coming out of the fog, blood running down its face and matting its fur. Jenny squirmed against him and he tried to keep hold of her.

The wolfman came towards him, lips peeled back over its teeth.

"Shit," said Alex and turned, pulling Jenny to him and back, so that they were against the carriage. The wolfman stopped in front of him and licked its lips. Bloody saliva dripped down onto the matted, wet fur of its chest.

There was nothing to do, no way out. Jenny moved against him, squirming as if to get away and caught the leg of his trousers. He heard change jingle and reached for it. A handful of coins, nothing more, no real weapon. But did he need one, or just a distraction?

The wolfman stepped forward and Alex could smell him, an awful meaty aroma that made him want to be sick again.

"Hey, Johnny," he said and the wolfman cocked its head to one side, glaring at him with its one remaining eye. "Yeah, Johnny, I've got some change for you."

Alex flung the coins at the wolfman's face and, with a howl, it brought up a huge forearm to shield it.

"Let's go," Alex shouted, moving to his left and grabbing Jenny under her arm, meaning to pull her with him. She'd been leaning on him and simply stumbled when he moved, sliding down his side. He tried to grab her tighter, but couldn't. She fell to the ground and he reached for her. The wolfman growled, deep in its throat.

"We have to go, Jenny," Alex said.

She looked at him, the whites of her eyes turning redder as he watched. Her blonde hair seemed to be growing darker and thicker by the second, getting coarser.

The wolfman growled again and as Alex looked up it lunged for his head.

Fogbound From Five

4

ADRIAN CHAMBERLIN

Kriegsmaterial

"Only be sure that thou eat not the blood: for the blood is the life; and thou mayest not eat the life with the flesh."
Deuteronomy 12.23

"*A little mist*" *you call it? No. This fog is a sign. It is identical to the mist that followed us on the cattle trucks that January night. Sixty years ago, and the memory is fresh. A memory I would gladly tear from my mind were I able. But, some things we shouldn't be allowed to forget...*

You must forgive me if I seem over excited. But this fog, here in London! The city that stood alone against Nazi evil. It is a sign, I am certain!

What's that? An explanation you require? Well, I do not think the train will be going anywhere for a while. We have time. Perhaps more time than you realise...

You know of Auschwitz-Birkenau. You know of the crimes committed there. The name Mengele is familiar to you, yes? His "experiments"? The very name sends a chill down your spine. As it should. For there was another experiment conducted in Block Ten at Birkenau, one that has been untold. Even the SS denied its existence.

You hear much of the cattle trucks on their way to the death camps. But you hear nothing of the return journeys. What do those trucks carry when they leave? A question few think to ask, because the final destination is all that matters...

This is my story. A story which perhaps will have no ending.

"Jew scum!"

A child's voice; the owner was probably eight or nine years old. The gleeful taunt was accompanied by the thud of something striking the wooden ribs of the cattle truck. To Samuel Wieck it sounded like a football, and he felt a fresh pang stab him in the heart. Of all the privations he had suffered, the simple sound of a ball kicked by a child his own age suddenly felt the worst of all.

How long is it since I last kicked a ball with friends? he wondered. *Would the boy outside play with me if he didn't know I was a Jew? But then, would he play with me if he knew what I have done?*

"Jewish bastards! You'll be turned into soap!" Another voice, another child. Samuel wasn't certain if it was the hatred spewed from the unseen children that made his fellow passengers groan, or the words themselves. The moans reverberated around him, faint and weak as the travellers. They faded, as though soaked into the soiled straw.

Samuel squirmed with the realisation that the sodden mass he had been slumped in was warmer. Now there was warmth encroaching upon him he realised just how cold the railway carriage was. Even colder than the corner of the barracks he shared with the other children. Even colder than Block Ten.

The smell was acrid, sharper than the urine that had accompanied their journey east for the last six hours. Coppery. The woman opposite him had not stirred, save for the contractions in her belly. Winter sunlight fought the fog successfully; from a gap in the warped slats behind him it broke through the mist and splashed across her face.

Her eyes stared back at his with no awareness, no recognition. Sightless. He saw a flash of rusted steel on the straw, then the sunlight disappeared back into the fog and the air felt thicker, more suffocating. The blood soaked into his trousers but he had not the strength to move himself. He could not even bring himself to pick up the nail the woman had used to open her wrists.

Jewish bastards! You'll be turned into soap!

It was a measure of the horrors they had endured that none had the energy or spirit to cry out "we have left Birkenau, stupid children! We have survived!"

No, it's because we suspect there are worse horrors to come, he told himself. *Perhaps worse than being turned into soap...*

The children's taunts ceased. Had they realised their mistake? Or was the abrupt silence because they knew the next destination of the train?

The woman in front of Samuel had already reached her destination. The unborn child...was it fathered by one of the SS guards or the *Kapos*? How had she hidden the nail used to kill herself? Samuel didn't know.

Does it matter, anyway? We're all dead, one way or another.

The train picked up speed; fresh, colder air slipped through the cracked panelling. Samuel shrank further into the corner, his arms crossed over his chest. Occasionally he would pick at the scabs on his arms through the ragged material of the striped shirt. The pain kept him alert; awake and focussed. His fellow passengers had begun to succumb to the cold. Some had fallen into the deep sleep that was the inmates' only escape from the camp. He could see hints of smiles on some of the sleeping faces. Perhaps they dreamed of food. That was a common dream, one they had all shared at one time or another.

Samuel had not dreamed of food for a long time. Not since Block Ten.

In addition to gentle snoring, Samuel could hear the rhythmic sound of wheels on rails; a sound that on first hearing, from the station at Lodz a year and a lifetime ago, had lulled his exhausted body to sleep with the memory of family holidays to the coast. The differences later had jerked him awake, screaming. The poor suspension of the four-wheeled cart, the shrieking of the rusted couplings, the slamming of bumper against bumper when the train negotiated poorly-maintained tracks and sidings - all brought home the difference between the luxurious carriages of the past and the cattle freight wagon he travelled in now.

And no mama or papa. He was surprised that he felt no grief at the time, but Mr Matathias said it was a blessing.

Will I feel it later? Samuel had asked as the sliding doors closed on them. Was it delayed by the shock of what he had seen happen in the Ghetto? Would the grief come for him later?

Mr Matathias had not replied. Samuel had known then. Even before they boarded the trains at Lodz they had suspected. The lies of resettlement in the east had not been believed by any of them, but few took seriously the rumours in the Ghetto of the killing camps, despite Mr Matathias's pleas.

I have seen them, the stranger from the east said to whoever would listen. *I have ridden the cattle trains to places whose names will be synonymous with human evil. Sobibor, Belsen, Majdanek, Treblinka...*

No, it was too outlandish to contemplate. Besides, if Mr Matathias had been to these places, how had he survived? His accent was suspiciously Russian-sounding. Ukrainian maybe, but still: a strong possibility that this shoemaker was from the Bolshevik country. Why should they believe him? Why had he returned?

You would not believe me if you knew. Suffice to say, you must listen to me. Do not board the trains. Hide yourselves. Survive. For the worst is yet to come. The small village near Krakow, the camp there...

The welcome on the railway tracks between the Auschwitz and Birkenau camps that November morning - the section of railroad known as the *Judenrampe* - proved Mr Matathias to be correct and revealed the lie of the Germans. The suitcases discarded, thrown with contempt by the *Kapos* to one side for raiding later; the barking of the dogs, jaws snapping at the arrivals' heels; the beatings from fists and clubs to force them into line; then the arrival of the selectors.

Black-uniformed shapes emerged from the mist like nightmares, the Death's Head on their caps a promise of things to come. A flick of a riding crop or a finger to indicate left or right - left to the showers, right to hard labour that was a more lingering death.

And then the figure in white. *Der Weiße Engel*, someone had muttered. To Samuel's eyes the man did indeed look like a white angel, with his outstretched arms and laboratory coat fluttering in the breeze as he directed his charges left and right. Slightly built, a well-scrubbed face with not a single hair out of place. He had a gentle smile for the children, particularly the twins, but that smile never reached his eyes. Even Samuel was startled by the man's stare. They were dead eyes, no humanity within them.

Proved when Mrs Herzburg refused to be separated from Rebecca, scratching the face of the SS man who forced the thirteen year old to the left hand line. The Luger came from nowhere: a crack split the morning air and a small hole appeared in the mother's forehead. Another shot, this time to the daughter. Twitching bodies bled their last on the *Judenrampe*, faded into the fog as Samuel looked once over his shoulder before he joined the right hand group.

Such was the welcome to Auschwitz-Birkenau by Joseph Mengele.

But we survived. The carriage they were on now was driving away from Auschwitz-Birkenau. And Mr Matathias was with them. A year in the camps soon taught them that he was not to be distrusted or reviled as a Bolshevik: they had others to fear. But, with the exception of Samuel, they still they kept their distance, for this man had an unsettling quality. Mr Matathias's bearing was not one of despair, but of humble endurance - as though his suffering was a penance to be rightly born. Only then did the fellow detainees believe his tales of survival, for only one who had witnessed and lived through such horrors could endure. And yet...

Even the guards left him alone. It was whispered, at night when the ice froze on the windows and the rats gnawed the bloodstained clogs of those ordered to dispose of the bodies, that even the SS were scared of Mr Matathias. Not once had a guard or trustee raised his voice to the enigmatic shoemaker; no whips were raised, no threats uttered. He was granted no special favours. There were no extra rations nor light duties, but it was obvious that the masters of the death camp did not know quite how to deal with Mr Matathias. Maybe there was truth to his tales after all?

"Is this how you returned from Treblinka, Mr Matathias?" The words didn't sound Samuel's own. His voice had changed so much; hoarse from occasional screams, wavering because of the constant fear that ensured he never spoke in more than a whisper within earshot of the *Kapos* or the SS guards. He tried to be brave, he tried *so* hard. Mr Matathias's courage was an example to them all, but none of them could match it.

For surely, courage that limitless could not be human.

"No, Samuel." Mr Matathias's buttery tones voice filled the cattle truck with warmth. The detainees' attention shifted from their fear and misery to the man who spoke. Like a candle in the darkness, his presence, his voice, brought comfort and hope. Fleeting, yes; but all the more precious for that.

"I took a different path. This…this is new to me."

"It must be over, surely?" A younger man's voice. Samuel recognised Hans Scholl's voice: the office worker from Hamburg, at one time the most optimistic of them all. The slightly built clerk had ridden the carriage from Lodz with hope and a forced jollity that only Samuel and Mr Matathias had not partaken of. Self-delusion that had shattered upon arrival at the *Judenrampe*.

"We are not being transported to a new work detail. The bombing flights have increased. My last work detail was at the armaments factory, and I saw Spitfires on strafing runs there. The bombers followed, but I don't think they managed to destroy the tracks…Germany is losing the war," Mr Scholl continued. "The Nazis don't want us to fall into the hands of the Russians, for the world to witness their crime. That is the only explanation for our movement, surely?"

Surely…Mr Scholl's favourite word, Samuel thought. *Always with an inflection, trying to convince himself as well as us…*

"Then why not the whole camp?" Mr Matathias said gently. "Each truck can hold over one hundred people - yet you saw this morning that only four carriages were connected. Only a few of us here, so...*what is in the others?"*

No-one answered. Some had already guessed, Samuel amongst them. As the train eased away from the *Judenrampe* the smell of the tender's burning coal could not hide the damp stink of human excreta that permeated the freight wagons. And from the carriage behind them had come something else: the unmistakeable stench of burned flesh and scorched bone.

"Disposal. We are being sent somewhere else to be disposed of."

Samuel glanced at the shadowed corpse of the pregnant woman and shuddered. Disposed of, but not by the "traditional" method. The stink of burning corpses was one of the few ever-present odours in the camps: with the introduction of the cremation pits to ease the burden placed upon the already overworked crematoria the stink leeched into every stone of the complex, every corner of the huts, settled into the fabric of the prisoner uniforms. Each night, upon their return from the burning fields, the clogs of the *Sonderkommandos* were coated in black ash and the soles spread a sticky tar-like substance; trailing the stink of extermination into the barracks of the living, an ever-present reminder of what awaited them all.

Even himself. Samuel knew to be one of "Mengele's children" was no guarantee of survival. If the experiments didn't kill them, the showers awaited. How he had deceived himself, believing he was one of the favoured! To think of what he had done to Franz…he shuddered.

"No. I do not believe it." Mr Scholl's head shook frantically. "You saw the looks on the guards when they forced us in. They were terrified of something. Whatever it is, it must work in our favour, surely? *Surely?*"

Silence greeted his words. Samuel saw Mr Scholl's Adam's apple jerk up and down his scrawny throat with each nervous swallow, fearful that Mr Matathias had no answer. Mr Matathias, the survivor of countless death camps; he must know what awaited them! But the corpse of the pregnant lady before him - which they all *must* be aware of – was proof that something terrible was coming.

Silence gave way to the rattle of the couplings, the hiss of steam as the locomotive was fed fresh fuel to power it up the slope. Samuel felt the flooring tilt and more blood, cool and viscous, pooled around his ankles. The tracks must be on a steep incline, for the train was slowing. The bank of freezing fog lowered and the winter sun came through the warped slats once more, illuminating the frightened faces of Samuel's fellow travellers.

Only Mr Matathias's features betrayed no fear. Impassive, emotionless, as though carved from stone. The stubble of his shaved scalp gleamed a cold, battleship grey in the light. Only his eyes, a striking, sapphire blue, indicated the warmth and humanity of this mysterious man from the east. They flashed in Samuel's direction.

"Once, I was forced onto a train such as this. Along with several others, pulled from the gas chamber at the very last moment. Told by the guards that we were free to go. The relief was indescribable - we even forced the memory of those who did not accompany us from our minds, so overjoyed were we by our reprieve.

"Instead, the train returned to the camp. We did not know this until we arrived at Treblinka once more, and were forced once again into the showers. It was an experiment, I learned later. An experiment in the physiological effects of hope. How quickly the human succumbs to death when he or she has had hopes raised in this manner."

Samuel heard some shocked gasps. He said nothing. The question was raised again: *how did you survive?*

He could see it in the sunset-illuminated eyes of the passengers. Some actually began to shuffle away from Mr Matathias, while Samuel continued to worry the needle marks in his arms.

"I do not need to tell you the effects this had on us. But this is not one of those trains. No, we are here for something else. Mr Scholl, you said the guards were terrified. Indeed they were. But what of?

"You ask me how did I survive? You must also answer that question. Each of you has more than mere *will* to survive. You have survived the worst years of the death camp. That ability, that *will* to survive is something the Nazis wish to quantify, to experiment upon. How can they? How can you measure the human spirit?"

"And you, Matathias?" a gruff voice came from the shadows, full of distrust and suspicion. "Your 'ability' to survive is greater than ours. No-one survives the shower rooms of Treblinka; yet you visited twice. What have you not told us? Huh! Maybe this is another experiment in 'hope'? You've been placed here to give us that, proof that one can survive the extermination camps! A sick joke!"

Samuel recognised the wizened features of Michael Volmar. The plumber from Hamburg, who had suffered more than anyone on his flight. The hardest of them all, who had nothing left to live for but the desire to see the end of Nazi rule. Samuel had watched him work with the other *Sonderkommandos,* saw the dispassionate way in which he despatched the corpses as though they were sacks of rubbish. Hatred gave the plumber the will to survive, but his humanity had gone, burned out of him by the tanks that had destroyed his home. Hope for vengeance, to see the Nazis crushed as they had crushed his wife and two daughters under the hells of their jackboots.

Matathias shook his head. "Ask yourself what is in the other carriages. Ask yourself why the guards are so terrified. They are scared of us, and our ability to survive...

"Only someone as inhuman as Mengele could possibly believe that the human spirit is…scientifically measureable. That it can be extracted, synthesised. It was a fictional vampire who perverted the line from Deuteronomy, and said 'the blood is the life'. But a real-life monster believed it. Acted upon it."

Samuel froze. His fingers halted in their worrying of the needle marks in his arms.

Mr Matathias stared at Samuel, then extended his own arms. All craned forwards to see. The marks on the shoemaker's arms were invisible, but Samuel was certain that Mengele had taken blood from him also. Why were there no marks on him?

"The blood is the life," Mr Matathias whispered. "He has taken blood from all of us, but me...he bled me dry. When he saw how quickly my cuts healed, how clean and unmarked was my flesh, he no longer needed your blood."

He bled you dry...and yet you still live! You walk with blood in your veins, life in your heart, and no marks upon your flesh. Now Samuel understood how Mr Matathias had survived the previous death camps.

Ahasuerus! It was beyond belief; yet as with all events that test man's sanity, the clues were right in front of us. The legend of the Wandering Jew is one that few know of these days. Ahasuerus, a porter in the service of Pilate, cursed by Jesus Christ to walk the Earth until the Second Coming for the crime of laughing at the Christian messiah and mocking his slow walk to Golgotha. In some versions of the legend he is a shoemaker...and that is the trade Mr Matathias claimed to have. His accent, strangely Slavic to our ears, was the voice of one who has travelled through many lands and spoken many languages.

All versions of the legend say he repented of his sins and was baptized Catholic. That is not the case. Matathias maintained his faith to the end. He had a mission, one that in many ways is more terrible than the ennui and rootlessness Christ forced him to endure.

And the Nazis believed. I often wonder what their faces looked like as he rose from the crematoria, fully fleshed and untouched by the flames like a phoenix! What fear they must have felt in the face of one they regarded as subhuman. But were they humbled? Did they repent? No. They merely found a new purpose for him...and even then, when they had exhausted all scientific endeavours upon him and he believed they could do no more, Mengele found a new use for what came from him...a military one.

That morning, after we loaded the rear wagons I saw crates loaded onto the final wagon. I thought it strange the Sonderkommandos or even the Kapos were forbidden to load them. The White Angel insisted he supervise the loading himself...each crate was labelled Dringend! Kriegsmaterial! - Urgent! War Material! *I wondered what was in them.*

For in Block Ten, I saw that stencilled on packages that contained organs and body parts. They would courier those parcels to the anthropological department at Berlin-Dahlem, they would never entrust them to the cattle trucks. So why, you may ask, were these packages travelling with us?

"We're stopping." Samuel looked up. "Can you feel it? The train is slowing. Why are they stopping? We've only been travelling a few hours!"

Mr Matathias cocked his head, listening closely to the nearest gap in the slats. They could all hear it now. Rumbling, like giant hornets in the air.

"Aeroplanes," Mr Matathias said. "They're cl - "

Rumbling gave way to thunder and lightning. Fire lit up the slats and holes opened in the roof. Steel hornets rained into the compartment, churned up the floorboards and peppered the sleepers. Mr Scholl screamed and beat a retreat to the far corner of the carriage, his clogs hammering on the floor. A crash and a squeal from the couplings, grinding from the bumpers and the carriages shuddered to a halt. The timbers rattled, the travellers shook and grabbed each other for purchase.

The rumbling faded, but Samuel kept his head between his knees, his arms clasped around Mr Matathias. He had heard that the fighter escorts of the bombers would come back for another strafing run, and...

"It's okay, Samuel. They've gone."

He realised he was trembling. He gritted his teeth, tears forming in his eyes. Once again, he had lacked courage. Once again, Mr Matathias had shown what bravery truly was. The shoemaker had not moved from his vantage point, had not recoiled from the bullets or splinters. Not a cry or a groan of pain from his lips joined those of the fellow passengers. Mr Scholl's clogs were still hammering on the floor, though; Samuel stared at them, fascinated by the fresh pool of scarlet that surrounded the drumming heels. Then he saw more blood, this time from Mr Matathias. He saw the wounds in Mr Matathias's chest, saw the white hint of rib and bullet-ridden lumps of blue organ. Then Mr Matathias pulled the tattered remnants of his shirt over the wounds, so as to hide them from sight. The blood ceased to flow. Samuel could not take his eyes away. He cocked his head, heard a sound unlike any he had heard before. Like the tearing of flesh, but...*in reverse*. As though muscle and skin were knitting, becoming hole once more.

Mr Scholl's feet ceased their death dance.

"I know your other name now. We thought you were a legend, a myth…"

"I am here to bear witness. To the crimes of evil men, and to the survival of the Children of Israel. I cannot be killed until He comes again, but make no mistake: I feel pain. Physical agony from the tortures and the fires of the Nazis. Spiritual agony from the sight of the Children of Israel, my people, being eradicated from existence. And of the depths to which they will sink to survive."

His eyes burned into Samuel's.

You know? But surely, you cannot judge me on that! You do what you can to survive…

"What crap is this?" Mr Volmar spat. "We've got no time for fairy tales! You're not another of Mengele's experime - "

Now new sounds filled the evening air. Distant gunfire, the roar of explosives. The hum of military vehicles, the crushing of frozen undergrowth and shattered tree trunks beneath tank treads. Mr Volmar's eyes blazed. He pushed past Mr Matathias and peered through the viewing hole.

"Russians!"

The travellers waited, rapid breaths misting in the truck, for the sliding doors to open and the order *Raus! Raus!* from their captors. Would the Germans shoot them now, or leave them to the Russians?

Small arms fire surrounded them. The clatter of machine guns was accompanied by the cries of their guards. Terror filled their voices. Samuel saw Mr Volmar grin.

"Not real soldiers, are you lads? Not like your pals in the Waffen SS. Go on, run. Fuck off while you can." His eyes narrowed. "I don't give anything for our own hopes with the Ivans. There's a forest a mile or so away. I say we get out now, take our chances."

"Do you know where we are?" Samuel asked.

"Not far from the armaments factory Scholl talked about. Looks like the Russians are finishing the job the British bombers started." He grinned, a wolfish snarl as he pulled at the slats. "Give me a hand, Matathias. Samuel, you too."

Planks splintered and twisted under the plumber's grip. He tossed the pieces to one side.

"Armaments factory," the man known as Mr Matathias said. "That was our destination."

"What?"

"Scholl said it had been bombed once before." The words were hard to hear over Mr Volmar's enthusiastic destruction of the boxcar's slats. Samuel opened his mouth to speak when a louder noise made all of them freeze.

Hammering of bone on wood. Splintering, cracking noises, far more powerful than the noises created by the plumber.

Samuel looked behind him. The far wall was mostly intact, save for the bullet holes from the strafing planes. The noise told him that it was the wall of the adjoining boxcar that was being destroyed. The force was such that the timbers of their own carriage shivered. The power behind the pummelling was too energetic, too powerful, to belong to fellow detainees from the camp. He glanced back to the man known as Mr Matathias, with eyes rounded by fresh terror. Mr Matathias looked back at him, with sadness and...*awareness,* realised Samuel. *He knows what it is!*

Mr Matathias got to his feet. Outside they could hear cries of terror, in German and Russian accents. The guns fell silent.

Each truck can hold over one hundred people - yet you saw this morning that only four carriages were connected. Only twenty of us here, so...what is in the others?

Disposal...

"Michael Volmar. You are *Sonderkommando*. What was it that could not be destroyed in the crematoria or the fire pits?"

A blank expression answered him.

"Quickly, man! What could not be destroyed?"

"N...nothing. *Everything* was destroyed! Well, almost everything..." his eyes locked on the rattling wall.

The pounding upon the boxcar's wall was rhythmic, the sound of a man beating the wood with two hands. Yet it was not the meaty *thud* of human fists on wood; Samuel had heard, and indeed felt, the pounding of fists upon defenceless bodies to know that there was no meat on the appendages that broke the wood.

"Bones..." the plumber breathed. "We asked for a bone crusher...the skeletons were too hard for us to break, we had not the strength..."

Mr Matathias's eyes, so pure and blue, filled with warmth, humanity and quiet courage, took on an expression Samuel had never seen before. For the first time, there was terror in the immortal's eyes.

"Crates...labelled *Urgent! War Materials!* Were there 'Fragile' markings on them also?"

Samuel frowned. "I'm not sure...there were 'Fragile' markings on some of the crates, but they were kept separate from the others. They contained glass vessels, I think. Blood samples, probably. Why is this.."

The blood is the life...he bled me dry...

"No," Samuel said in a hoarse voice. "No, they couldn't. Not even *they* would do such a thing..."

The sound of rapidly-advancing boot heels, crunching on frozen snow, was followed by automatic gunfire. Bullets ploughed into the slats of the box wagon and ricocheted off the things that were breaking into it.

The sound of lead striking bone filled Samuel's ears. Through the fresh holes in the slats, he caught a glimpse of a charred limb swinging at the SS guard's pistol, like a lightning-struck branch falling from a blasted oak.

It's not from a tree, he realised with horror. *And the charring, the scorching, is from the crematoria, not lightning...*

The Luger's firing pin clicked on empty chambers before falling from the soldier's hand. The sound of the weapon striking the rails was muffled by the scream of its owner.

Samuel shrank away from the slats, no longer anxious to escape. Screams like this he had heard before, in Block Ten: the barely human cry of one who was faced with something far more terrifying than the casual, professional slaughter of the death camp.

Barely human. He looked to his companion, to the one who called himself Mr Matathias. The stranger's eyes burned with such rage, such inhuman malevolence, that Samuel wilted under the glare. So much so he returned to the slats, hoping - he never prayed anymore – that Mr Matathias's rage was directed against the things outside the box car and not himself.

But maybe both, he thought. *He has walked the Earth for almost two thousand years. He knows evil. He knows what I did in Block Ten...* Samuel focussed on the slaughter outside. What he saw took his breath away.

Steam rose from below, accompanied by the stink of shredded organs. The white cloud of vapour from the SS guard's disembowelment, as thick as the fog that had followed them from the camp, obscured Samuel's view; he had the impression of animated blackened bones, thrashing as though they were going under the bone crusher Mr Volmar had referred to.

But these were not being destroyed. The blood splattered from its rending appendages told Samuel these were doing the destroying. When the guard's writhing ceased, and his only movements were the jetting of hot blood on the frozen rails, the creature rose. The black dome of its skull was misshapen, swollen with fractures that had not been allowed to heal before death. The lower jaw was missing, but the few remaining teeth in the upper mandible made identification easy. Too easy for Samuel; guilt followed his recognition of Franz's overbite and brought its own agony.

The creature reached its hands towards the slats, blood dripping from its outstretched, skeletal fingertips. Samuel felt his heart pound, for this action was not a threatening one. Those fleshless claws did not want to rend or tear his flesh. They wanted to hold him for comfort, for reassurance, just as they had done in Block Ten.

Samuel's eyes were blurred with tears. Even now, the child did not remember what Samuel had done to it. Even now it trusted him, its eyeless sockets seeing him as the big brother who had befriended it in Block Ten when it was human.

It could not reach, however; the open slats were too high for a child's reach. If the creature had vocal cords or lips it would have howled its despair to the winter sky. It had nothing to articulate its grief.

Grief turned back to rage. The skeletal fingers turned inwards, formed fists with a scrape of bone against bone. Fresh, pure white revealed itself as charred flakes fell to the ground like black snow. Samuel held his breath, awaiting the assault upon the wooden wall. He blinked his tears away and braced himself.

Whatever happens now, I deserve it. You trusted me, Franz, and I betrayed that trust. In that moment he felt more alone than ever before in his short life. Perhaps this was how his countrymen felt when they were herded into the showers and the gas pellets fell into the mesh pillars. Surrounded by people and yet completely alone, as are all who face death. Not even the company of Mr Matathias, the man who walked always with death but never experienced it, registered. Samuel took a deep breath and stared into the far distance.

The sun was just below the gap in the hills, bleeding red onto the snow coated summits; it trickled downwards, soaking the barren fields and the shattered fortifications of the armaments factory that Scholl had spoken of. Clouds of white smoke from the shelled industrial units replaced the fog from the lower slopes, infusing the winter air with the smell of chemical fire. Samuel's nostrils flared, the aroma almost pleasing in comparison to that of the plumes that belched constantly from the camp's crematoria towers.

He heard the thunder of the tanks, saw the swivelling of turrets and the tongues of flame from the barrels of their guns; the red star on the turrets glowed ruby in the light from the reflected fires. Vengeance from Stalin - or Hell itself?

*No difference, if Mr Volmar is to be believed...*but even the soldiers of the feared Red Army hesitated to approach the motionless train. Samuel almost smiled as the skeletal figure turned from the box wagon and faced the tanks.

He saw now Franz was not alone. Others of the *Kriegsmaterial* had finished their slaughter of the SS guards and now turned their attention from their still-living Jewish brethren.

"The blood is the life." Samuel almost smiled. Mengele's children – the young and the old, infants and parents alike - had been a greater success than the White Angel could have dreamed, and a crueller weapon could not have been invented. The dead of Birkenau, reanimated by the blood of the shoemaker who had laughed at Christ on the way to Golgotha.

Samuel heard weeping. Sounds he thought the *Sonderkommando* was incapable of making. He turned and stared at Mr Volmar.

"How could you, Matathias? How could you let them take your blood? In the name of God, did you not know what it would be used for?"

Matathias shook his head. "Only this day did I realise. War Materials…I thought it impossible, that the curse of my life was my own. Only true evil could think to pervert my curse, to use it for its own ends."

Samuel wondered if the shoddy loading was deliberate. Crates of fragile glassware, filled with blood drained from the inmates of Block Ten, guaranteed to shatter and spill into the crates marked *Kriegsmaterial* at the slightest collision.

Gunfire. Samuel turned back, stared with fascination at the bullets that tore through the walking frameworks of the dead. Pieces of bone splintered and flew to the ground, but their approach was not halted. The empty shells of humanity strode towards Stalin's soldiers, their march as relentless and remorseless as death's itself.

The firing of automatic rifles faded, replaced by the sound of worn boots crunching through frozen snow as their owners beat a frantic retreat; then replaced with the roar of tank engines and the clatter of metal tracks as the T-34s took their place.

All six tanks formed a semi circle facing Samuel's side of the box wagon. Six turrets swivelled in his direction. Six barrels aimed at the approaching mass of charred and scorched skeletal remains. Samuel's fingers tightened on the broken slats. He didn't feel the splinters gouge his flesh, was unaware of his blood trickling through his fingers. His eyes were riveted on the gun barrels. All six guns would tear through the *Kriegsmaterial*, but the shells wouldn't stop there.

Jewish bastards! You'll be turned into soap!

Samuel smiled grimly. "No. Still wrong. *I will survive.*" He reached for Mr Matathias's hand and held it. His fingers dug into Mr Matathias's flesh.

In the instant the blackness of the six barrels gave birth to fire, Samuel felt Mr Matathias pull his hand away. A flinch, a reactive movement. But not one of fear.

One of disgust. Samuel turned, too late to see Mr Matathias's face as he pulled away, too late to ask why he was to be denied human comfort; but he suspected.

The world exploded into a swirling sculpture of fog, snow, blood and fire. The box wagon disintegrated. Splinters of wood tore through Samuel's face, taking his eyes and smashing the teeth from his mouth. He fell to the floor in a welter of blood and torn flesh, too stunned for the pain to register. He didn't see the shards of blackened *Kriegsmaterial* that followed, but he felt them.

He felt the pieces of his Block Ten companions slice through his body, tearing his abdomen and sloughing the flesh from his bones. Perhaps it was the rocking of the carriage's axles and wheels on the tracks, but it felt to Samuel Wieck that the pieces of disintegrated bone embedded in his ravaged body were moving…

I did not see the end of the war. The liberation of the camps, the defeat of Nazism, the Allies' betrayal of Poland; I witnessed none of those. When the Soviets saw how quickly I healed I did not even spend any time in their "resettlement" camps. My life consisted of blindfolded journeys from one military establishment to another. Blood was taken from me, but they did not drain me as Mengele drained Mr Matathias. Did my blood have the same power as his? I do not know. I suspect not, for the Cold War would have a markedly different conclusion, would it not?

After my medical uses were exhausted I was sent to the Gulags. It was there that I grew to manhood. I never spent much time in each one, though. As soon as my fellow inmates heard of my history, I became an icon, a symbol of hope to the oppressed. The authorities feared that. It is ironic that I witnessed some of the most terrible penal institutions of the post war period: just as Mr Matathias experienced camps whose names became bywords for human evil, I lived in camps that, although not built to wipe us from the face of the Earth, certainly proved the Soviets treated their "undesirables" with the same brutality and contempt as the Nazis.

"The blood is the life," Mr Matathias said. His blood gave some form of life to the Kriegsmaterial - to this day I do not know what the Soviets did with

the remnants. Are they still alive, in specimen jars in some long-forgotten Soviet laboratory? Do the new criminal masters of Russia have plans for them? Or did the second life within their bones evaporate with the flames the Red Army spat upon them after the shelling?

And myself? How did I survive? Why am I still alive? I am an old man now, yet my appearance to you is that of a man aged thirty, just as Mr Matathias appeared to us.

He told me his role is to bear witness to the evils of mankind - to experience it first hand - while he awaits the Second Coming. Only with the return of Christ, he believed, will his curse be ended. I have not seen him since that fog-bound sunset on the Birkenau train, but I will continue to search for him.

I believe that I too am ordained to bear witness to the evil of man. I sense terrible times ahead; far worse than the crimes against humanity of the twentieth century. And I know that I will experience them. I have no hopes nor pleasant memories to help me endure. The most powerful memory of my life is Mr Matathias pulling his hand from me. Why? Was my crime so great?

In Auschwitz-Birkenau, you did what you had to survive. Perhaps he had been immortal for too long. Perhaps he couldn't understand the depths to which starvation will make you sink. I am certain I was not the only one to eat meat in Block Ten. Even afterwards, when I was told what the meat was, and who it had come from...still I fed. I did not see it as my brother Franz, I saw it as food.

I travel the railways, seeking Mr Matathias still. I want to explain this to him, to find a way to end my suffering. We were parted on a night such as this. Maybe we'll meet again on such a night. Fog, train and London…it seems a sign.

For London is the city that stood alone against Nazi tyranny. The will to survive flows through its waterways and the stones of its buildings like blood. London understands the nature of sacrifice.

The blood is the life.

5

PETER MARK MAY

End of the Line

Gary Harrison managed to get on the last train home from London with forty-five seconds to spare before the carriage doors hissed shut. He staggered to an empty set of four seats and sat down with the contented grin of the half-pissed on his face.

He'd been out with the boys from the work: one last hurrah before the shit-hit-the-fan on Monday morning. BKR Banking, Gary's employer for the past ten years was on the full skids down to hell. Most of its employees - including Gary and his mates - would be getting their P45s on Massacre Monday, as they had all dubbed it.

Pub session had become Chinese meal, which led to a strip club and the exiting of ninety percent of the three hundred quid he had in his wallet at the start of the evening.

Tracey had not taken the news well, but he had long given up taking anything his wife said into consideration. Things at home were bad to put it mildly; she had been having an affair with the widowed plumber ten years Gary's senior, who lived across the street.

Apparently this fit forties man, with more hair and get up and go than Gary, had been cuckolding his wife's pipes for over a year now. Tracey was quite explicit in yelling at him during their daily arguments that Richard's todger (her exact terminology) was twice the length and girth of his.

Gary applauded Dick the Plumber for having at least one decent working tool in the box.

Things had come to a head in their marriage as Tracey had made a dramatic exit a month ago, dragging her leopard skin suitcases across the road for all of Bentley Drive to gawp through their net curtains at.

Dick the Plumber had opened the front door of his house, seen the suitcases and proceeded to tell Tracey to *fuck right off*, with a sneer that - as a fellow man - Gary gave kudos to.

Gary had smiled, pulled open the tab of his lager and sat down to watch a repeat of *Thunderbirds,* while the wife cried her eyes out, sitting on her suitcase on the grass verge outside.

Gary had waited for the fiftieth combination of knocks and rings on the doorbell before taking his key out of the lock and unbolting the latches. He didn't wait for her cries of sorrow or begs of marital mercy; he just sat down with another can of lager and watched an old *Space 1999* episode next.

A stop at a station still inside Greater London caused him to jolt awake. The pints of beer were pressing hard on his bladder now, so he staggered up and headed for the nearest loo.

He sat down and pissed like a girl, because of his un-sober legs and the jolting train movements as it raced along the tracks.

Gary Harrison let out a sigh as the urine finally consented to flow. He smiled contently and laid his head against the loo wall and was asleep before the last drop had dripped.

Gary came too three hours later with a mild headache, a mouth like a birdcage and very cold legs and groin.

"Wadda fuck stunt, eh?" he mumbled incoherently, blinking his eyes and trying to remember where he bloody was.

"Oh shit," He spoke over dry cigar tasting lips, as he rose on pins-and-needles affected legs and realised the lavatory light was no longer on and the electric door was wide open.

He pulled up his pants and trousers and fumbled to pull his zip up and button in haste, hoping no one had seen him like this.

Gary imagined he would soon be the next mobile phone star of YouTube or have it posted on Facebook for all his mates to see.

He exited the lavatory and found that the train was now stationary and all the lights in the carriages were off. He wandered down the corridor into the carriage proper and bumped his elbow on a pole hidden by the darkness.

"Ow-*shit*," he hissed, while his eyes tried to adjust to the dark. *Where the hell am I, in the train depot or someplace?*

He made it to an electric door, put his cupped hands up to the glass and put his face closer to peer out. All he could see was darkness, a bit of track and a whole lot of fog.

"Oh great," Gary said loudly, rubbing his funny bone. He walked over to the door in the opposite side of the carriage.

With an extended bottom lip, he once again peered out of the dark confines of the train.

"More fog." But there were also the edges of a dark cantilever roof and smudges of strip lights and the grey concrete of a station platform. If there were any buildings, or people or station name signs; the fog was doing a great job of concealing them.

Gary wasn't sure if it was the night, his bladdered eyes or a tint in the glass, but the fog seemed to have a green tinge to it.

"Where the hell am I?" Gary pulled up his shirt and jacket cuffs; shocked that his illuminated watch read 3:33am. No taxi firm or buses would be running now: it looked like he had a cold night and long walk ahead of him.

He rubbed at his ever expanding forehead and pressed the button next to the door marked OPEN.

Nothing happened, so he pressed it again and again and again like it was from some eighties video game. He even pressed the CLOSE button twice, just in case, but still nothing happened.

"This ain't happening." He lent on the glass, the cold pane soothing his aching head.

Then he was off down the corridor through two open connecting doors into the next carriage. He went to the next station side door and pushed the

OPEN button, but nothing would happen. He peered out the window to see a scene much like the one from the other carriage. The only difference was that on the platform, lying on the stand-well-back-behind-the-yellow-line, was a lady's umbrella.

"The bloody electricity's been turned off." He edged himself back to stare down the centre aisle of the train. Turning his head from left to right he saw no sign of any other passengers, train staff or lights anywhere.

"How the hell am I gonna get off this train?" Gary's mind was flummoxed to panic levels; he was stuck on an electric train, with no electricity and was pretty darn sure that this wasn't his stop. He had obviously slept past his station, gone to the end of the line and the guard or driver had missed him and now he was stuck on the train.

Exhaling and rubbing his hand through his thinning scalp, Gary looked up in the semi-gloom and saw something that might just help.

IN CASE OF EMERGENCY BREAK GLASS AND PULL LEVER TO OPEN DOORS MANUALLY.

In a Perspex case above the door was a lever and an arrow pointing from NORMAL to RELEASE, it helpfully read.

Gary lent against the wall and tried to pull off one of his shoes, nearly fell and had to put his foot down to steady himself, but finally came up with it in his hand.

Putting his arm over his eyes and aiming his heel at the glass he whacked at it, but he closed his eyes at the last second and missed it completely.

He peeked with one eye open over his jacket sleeve and gave it a good hit this time. The glass cracked and broke with a satisfying sound and Gary tapped away five more time to make sure it was glass-free.

It was only when he was returning his shoe to his foot when he noticed another sign that read: £50 FINE FOR IMPROPER USAGE.

"*Now* you tell me." Gary Harrison whined and reached up to pull the lever. The door hissed open and went ten centimetres left before stopping. Gary moved forward, gripped the open gap of the door and with a little effort pushed it open enough to exit through.

Shuffling sidewards he stepped down onto the cold foggy platform and nearly threw up. There was an overpowering smell of hospitals in the air that the sealed train had kept from his nostrils.

Gary pulled a hanky from his trouser pocket and put it over his mouth: all thoughts of suing the train company for unlawful imprisonment had gone for the moment.

His flipping stomach settled and the disinfectant-like smell eased a little as his olfactory senses slowly got used to it. He moved in and down the station platform to find a name sign that read: Kendell Wood.

"Great the end of the line." The name of the station rang a bell because he saw it on the departure boards and on the in-train message screens every day. He was deep in-country now and at least seven stops away from home.

He followed the brick-walled station house, came to the exit and passed through into a waiting room-cum-ticket office.

His luck changed a little as the lights were still on and the doors to the station were wide open. The glow of a vending machine caught Gary's eye and he made a B-line for it. He took the hanky from his nose and mouth. The air still tasted of hospitals, but it was becoming bearable now.

He dug out some change and purchased a bottle of water, which fell to its opening slot with such a noise that Gary hadn't realised how quiet it was outside.

"It's the middle of the night," he chastised himself. He sucked on the refreshing water greedily. He polished off half the bottle, and then had to pop to the Men's toilet to the left of him to urinate again.

By habit he went into a cubicle, which had one frosted small window that was about shoulder level and looked out onto the front parking forecourt of the railway station.

As Gary finished and shook off, a shadow crossed the frosted window in the fog outside. Dark and distorted it passed, but spoke in a muffled woman's voice.

"Kee-rul eero – ssumneeda?"

Gary frowned at the Asian voice by the window, and then heard footsteps diminishing in sound as the person walked off.

"Bloody tourists," Gary muttered and left the toilets without washing his hands, sipping the water bottle again.

He rubbed his nose and went to stand at the station exit. The strange looking and smelling fog obscured most things. Connected to the station were a line of one storey brick shops; the first being a newsagents. Gary buttoned up his jacket against the night's chill air and followed the line of shops. A drycleaner's came next after the newsagents, then a florist's and then a taxi firm.

No lights were on, but a streetlamp above in the misty air gave enough illumination to read the sign in the window.

KENDELL WOOD TAXI SERVICE
OPEN 24/7 CALL OFFICE OR MOBILE
NUMBER BETWEEN THE HOURS OF 12-6AM

Gary pulled a hopeful face and grabbed his mobile from his outer jacket pocket.

"Bollocks." He swore looking at the dreaded words that were, NETWORK UNAVAILABLE.

"Shit." He swore again and kicked the nearest lamppost with the side of his shoe, as not to really hurt himself. He put the mobile phone away and headed off down the end of the curved car park/forecourt of the railway station.

Above him, attached to the lamppost, was a sign hidden by the fog that stated: DEMARCATION AREA ZULU.

Gary trudged to the end of the car park forecourt and looked left and right. He sniffed because of the cold, damp conditions and tried to think what he could do next.

Looking right he saw the road rise up into a humpback bridge that went over the railway tracks below before becoming shrouded in fog. To his left the road sloped a little downwards and disappeared around the edges of a three storey building.

He stuffed his hands in his pockets and tumbled his mobile over and over while his booze-addled brain tried to do an impression of his sober mind.

"*Think*," he whispered to himself, not wanting to startle himself with louder words. The place was dark, foggy and silent as the grave. *What do you expect for the middle of the bleeding night?* He chastised himself again.

He walked towards the large building, just for something to do; then his mind gave birth to a clever thought for once.

"Telephone box!" he stated loudly to the side of the dark windowed building. A sign on the corner bore the words Kendell Wood, twinned with Ste.Mere-Eglise and an arrow pointed towards the way he was heading.

There was bound to be a telephone box somewhere in this backwater shit-hole; so hands in pockets he began walking along the cold pavement that lead towards the village.

The large unknown building gave way to a one storey Spar shop and then a dark, locked up garage. No lights were on apart from the odd street lamp post above in the fog, its yellowed smudged illumination swirling above his head.

The lamp posts led his way as he walked, but all signs of buildings were left behind with the garage. Bramble covered fences were the only thing to the left of him and he could only see halfway across the road to the central white lane dividing lines. Beyond the fences were fields, but all Gary could see was ditches and the beginnings of wet muddy grass.

He was just *umm*ing and *arr*ing on whether to cross the road to see if he'd missed something, when the familiar sight of an old fashioned red telephone box loomed out of the mist ahead, just off the side of the pavement.

"Finally," he muttered, his luck changing at last. He fumbled in pockets and pulled out a selection of shrapnel, including at least three pound coins. He pulled open the door convinced it would be vandalised, but his faith in British youth was restored as everything looked in working order.

Gary fished the cold receiver from its cradle and put it to his ear, his first pound coin held between thumb and forefinger ready to put in the slot. The phone had no dial tone to it, but from it hissed a distant female voice.

"*Mi sono perso.*" The woman's voice repeated this over and over again, in what sounded to Gary like Italian.

"Do you speak English?" Gary said down the phone, wondering if someone from Italy had dialled this telephone box by accident.

"*Mi sono person, mi sono perso.*" The voice continued.

"Erm, *excusi*, can you put down your phono or I can't dial out. *Comprehendi?*" Gary asked, trying his best for Anglo-Italian relations.

"*Mi sono per -*"

"-Get off the fucking phone you stupid foreign bitch! I can't dial out until you put your stunting phone down." Gary's chance of a career in the diplomatic service, were abruptly over.

"*Mi sono perso.*"

Gary slammed the phone down on its cradle, nearly crying with rage and frustration at the situation he found himself in.

Gary stopped shaking, took a deep breath and mentally counted to ten. He'd only got up to eight before he grabbed the receiver again.

"*Mi sono perso,*" came the voice again, like an old vinyl record jumping back to say the same thing time after endless time.

Gary howled with rage and smashed the receiver against the rest of the phone fourteen times, until his hand stung and the black handset was broken in two and no longer working.

Gary barged his way out of the telephone box, bashing his left ankle against the door in his haste to depart. Cursing every swear word he could think of, he hobbled down the road again, hoping to find a hotel or at least another phone box in the village.

Behind him, in the field, a dark human shape moved out of the dense fog towards the fence and watched until Gary disappeared from sight.

At last he came to another building, a cottage with thatched roof and a small garden in front of it. The gate was open and on the path laid a child's stroller, turned on its side.

Gary sniffed and blew his nose with his hanky and moved on without stopping. The road grew thinner at this point, because he could just make out the dark wooden shape of one of those really old bus shelters across the road. He thrust his cold hands deeper into his pockets and walked on towards the village proper.

Inside the bus shelter something awoke from its slumber and moaned in low confused tones.

Gary soon came to more houses and ahead the road forked into two, around a concrete circle with a stepped dais and remembrance cross.

He continued on into the village on the left hand fork. Ahead to his left and right more houses and shops loomed into misty view and the orange smudged illuminations of lampposts seemed to come every twenty feet now.

The pavement bent round to the left; immediately off it was a large old coaching inn-cum-village pub. It had white walls and on the bend a large open arch led into a yard at the inn's side; with more old stable buildings - or guest rooms - beyond.

Gary walked past, then stopped, certain he'd caught sight of a person in his peripheral vision. He listened and heard the shuffling of feet coming from the inn's courtyard.

A cold chill raced down his spine, but he ignored it and quickly hurried back to the open archway. He was vindicated; as with the thick mist at the far end of the yard, at the corner of the inn was a figure.

"Hi there, don't suppose you've got a room for the night or a working telephone, do ya?"

The figure mumbled something softly, sounding like to Gary's ears that he/she had a scarf wrapped around their mouths or something.

"Sorry, I didn't quite catch that; what did you say again?" Gary moved closer and above him, fixed to the archway, a security lamp came on and illuminated the misty scene.

The figure at the corner of the inn was dressed in what looked like pyjamas to Gary, but had his head bowed and all features were still distorted by the fog.

"*Ekho khathi.*" The muffled voice spoke louder this time and raised his bowed head, as Gary got within a few feet of the stranger.

"What? Is this village the tourist capital of the world then?" Gary joked, but he didn't feel at all amused at hearing his third different language of the night.

"*Ekho khathi,*" repeated the man. With hunched shoulders and a head tilted down to one side he began to shuffle towards Gary.

"Doesn't anyone speak Eng-" Gary stopped in midsentence as the shuffling man came out of the mist at him and Gary saw his appearance clearly for the first time.

The man's face had somehow melted down from his forehead to his chin and his skin had taken the look of a piece of liver left out in the rain for two weeks. His large nose had melted down over his lips, so that the man had a small gap to the left and half a working mouth to the right. With skin that seemed to hang from his fingers, he reached out for Gary with a new single word.

"*Petheno.*"

Gary felt the melted man's creepy hands brush his back as he ducked, turned and ran out of the yard. He turned left and ran down the street past several shops. He ran around an army Landrover that lay on its side, halfway through the window of a small sports shop. Gary skidded to a halt in the road; ahead of him, coming out of the fog, shambled three more figures, one of which could only be a child.

He turned tail and ran back to the army vehicle and entered the shop through the window, his shoes crunching on broken glass. A light illuminated the till area, so Gary could see there were no people inside the crashed Landrover. He pulled out his mobile phone and used it as a small torch as he bent through the smashed windscreen, looking for any weapons that had been left behind.

Outside somewhere distant, he heard a faint but shrill scream of a frightened woman. Seeing no dropped guns, Gary retreated back into the shop and pocketed his phone again.

From outside the shop a collection of jumbled voices all speaking in different languages could be heard, getting closer and closer. Gary grabbed the first thing that came to hand - a hockey stick - and ran back around the till counter, trying to open the white door behind it.

"Fer-*fuck's*-sake." The locked door only rattled in its doorframe, but would not open. The maelstrom of foreign accents was louder now and feet, some bare, trod on the glass on the pavement outside the sports shop.

He ducked behind the counter and hid, gripping the hockey stick across his body like a comfort blanket.

Gary Harrison held his breath as best he could in his terrified state, as the melted faced creatures with foreign voices entered the shop. He looked around and on the shelf by his head, was open boxes of white and red cricket balls.

He had nowhere to hid or flee to, so instinct of a hundred generations of fighting Englishmen bubbled to the surface. He stood up, dropping the hockey stick and moved the boxes of cricket balls up upon the counter and began throwing them at the advancing shambling figures.

At first his panicked throws went wide, until a wickedly chucked white ball hit the child Shambler right were her nose had once been. Instead of bouncing off, the one-day-ball disappeared deep into the squashed pulp of her brain and she collapsed to the floor and lay there, unmoving.

Gary whooped with joy and began to throw the balls at the larger three adult targets. His next ball hit a woman on the side of her Flemish-speaking cheek, caving half of it in, as though her skull was made of peanut brittle.

When Gary reached down a few seconds later he found all his cricket-related ammo had been thrown, in his sick version of a coconut shy. Only one Shambler remained: the melted nose man-thing from the inn's courtyard.

Gary knelt down and picked up the hockey stick from its dropped position, just as Nose Man rounded the counter. Gary stood up and swung the hockey stick in an upward arc towards his attacker's chin. The plan went to pot, as Nose Man caught the hockey stick and pulled it from Gary's surprised hands.

"*Petheno*," mumbled Nose Man.

Gary threw the till at the Shambler; not waiting to see the outcome he ran around the other side of the counter. He grabbed a nine iron on his dash out of the shop and ran across the road, into a loading alley between a coffee shop and newsagents.

He ran straight into a female figure coming the other way down the dark fog-shrouded alleyway that ran behind the back-to-back shops.

With screams of terror they fell into a tangled, scared mess on the wet rubbish strewn cobbles.

Gary scrambled back on his bum, and then rose up over the female, ready to nine-iron her across the head.

"Please don't hit me, I'm an English girl, I ain't done nothin' wrong." Cried the woman on the alley floor; shadows covering her features.

"You're not foreign and manky looking then?" Gary stepped from foot to foot, still holding the golf club above his head.

"Nah, I'm Kylie Pickering. Wait." The girl sat up, a lighter flicked on and Gary could see a tanned pretty face of a girl in her late teens.

"What the hell is going on here?" Gary lowered the club to reach down to give the girl a hand rising to her feet.

"I dunno, but those things killed me bessie mate Carly. Have the Russians invaded or something? Or is it one of those Al-IKEA attacks?" The lighter went out and the scared wild-eyed girl's face disappeared back into the gloom.

"I ain't got a frigging clue, love." His hand was outstretched again to shake hers, now she was standing up. "I'm Gary, by the way."

"Gary behind you!" The words were so shrill it felt like his eardrums might burst.

He whirled round to find the Nose Man Shambler had caught up with him. Gary had no time to flee, so his body's survival instincts kicked in and he whacked the melted face thing in the side of the head with the golf club. There was a sickening crack as the nine-iron disappeared into the skull and lodged in the brain matter behind, the golf club pointing out of his left eye socket like an overexcited Dalek. The Shambler tottered backwards, taking Gary by surprise and pulling the golf club out of his hands.

Gary moved back next to Kylie and put a protective arm around her. They watched the Shambler crash into a wall. This caused its squashed eye to pop out onto its cheek and finally the creature fell into a heap and lay still.

"I think we better find somewhere safe to hole up - maybe find a landline telephone that works." Gary pushed Kylie into motion and they turned right at the crossroad into the alleyway.

"Yeah, 'cos my mobile phone ain't working either." Then the scared girl burst into spontaneous tears. Gary pulled her into a hug, and they stood wordlessly for a while, holding each other in the filth of the loading bays and misty back exits of shops.

"Come on," he lifted her chin with thumb and forefinger, "we can't stay out in this fog with those things about. We're too exposed."

"I know," she sniffed, wiping her eyes with the cuffs of her jacket.

"Look, you try the doors on that side and I'll try the ones on this side." He nodded left for her and pointed right for him.

"Okay." She sniffed and headed left across the back alley to the first door; while Gary headed to the right hand side.

The first shop Gary came to went down a smaller alleyway to a side door. He nervously fished out his mobile and used it as a makeshift torch to lead the way. He reached the side door and tried the handle, but it didn't budge an inch. Gary exhaled, not sure if it was relief because anything could be waiting for him inside or anger that it was locked.

His thoughts were interrupted by another shrill Kylie scream of terror, like a foghorn mixed by some mad DJ.

He came running out of the small alley to find Kylie shrieking her large lungs out by some bins as the crawling golf-nutted Shambler had one of her ankles in his floppy skinned grip.

With a roar of testosterone-fuelled rage Gary ran at the Shambler and booted the thing in the head like a goalie taking a goal kick. The Shambler's head left its shoulders and hit the nearby wall with a gloopy sounding splat and the golf club went rattling across the cobblers, causing an awful racket. With Kylie's screaming and the rest of the clamour, any nearby Shambler would be descending on them very soon.

"Come on," he said, grabbing her hand and pulling her down the alley further. Fortunately her survivor instincts clicked in and she ran with him. Further along and hidden before by two large wheelie bins was an open door to a shop, with a faint glow emanating from within.

Gary pushed Kylie gently behind him and they approached the open door, as quietly as her two inch heels could muster. Gary peeked around the door, which was next to a larger shuttered goods entrance.

Inside was a storeroom of some kind, filled with shadowy rectangles of machinery, boxes and other unknown supplies. The faint glow came from a doorway only a crack ajar, which probably lead into the front of the shop.

Kylie gripped his hand tightly, her red fake nails digging into his skin. The machinery appeared to be photocopiers of some hi-tech, elaborate design. There were mesh cages on wheels mostly filled with boxes and one filled with cardboard tubes of various shapes and lengths. A couple of chairs stood in front of switched off computers. As they entered further, they saw another dark doorway to their left.

Ignoring that door, they edged slowly towards the lit doorway ahead, Kylie's hot breath on Gary's neck, keeping eagle-eyes out for strange shapes or movements among the shadows.

By the door was a fire extinguisher, on a wall-mounted hook. Gary left Kylie behind a step and grabbed the extinguisher to use as a makeshift weapon: his third of this bizarre night.

He pulled the door open with the toe of his shoe to reveal a well lit shop beyond. Very hi-tech looking, with soft wall lights A brightly-illuminated counter was infront of the door in an L-shape, with an opening to the right. More computers, photocopiers and other stranger white plastic machinery lined the shop front. The walls were covered with pictures; prints, frames, posters, flyers, book covers, record covers and canvasses.

Kylie picked up a piece of stationery on the counter and read out: "Pollard and Yorque Designs."

Gary could see no Shamblers in the place, but rounded the counter to make sure. The shop was open and gave no real place for one of those creatures from the fog to hide. A quick check of the shop door found it was locked and covered with a roller-shutter door. The windows were exposed to the fog outside, but designs covered most of the window space. Seeing nothing moving outside, Gary headed back to the counter.

Gary rushed past her into the storeroom and shut and bolted the door they had entered through. Then jumped out of his skin, when the lights suddenly went on overhead.

He spun to see Kylie properly for the first time; in her short jacket, tight plunging top and mini-skirt give him an apologetic look. She was a tits and tan teenage temptress and even with her slightly orange face, she looked to Gary to be very desirable underneath all her layers of makeup.

Gary put his forefinger on his lips and then pointed towards the other side door they had not tried yet. Kylie sucked in her glossed lips and nodded like a loon, her brown hair moving a second after her head.

Gary hefted up the fire extinguisher and reached out for the door marked PRIVATE: STAFF ONLY. He took a deep breath and held it, then pulled the door open.

Inside was a chair; a table by a painted over double window, four tall thin lockers, a sink unit with a basin and a collection of mugs, sitting next to a kettle. A built in fridge and cupboards were underneath the basin and work surface. Another open door led off it and a loo could be plainly seen in the semi-darkness.

Gary switched on the light, just inside the door and had a quick peep inside the lavatory just to make sure.

"Fuck me, there is a God." Kylie stated, moving past Gary to enter the toilet and close the door behind her with a relieved sigh.

Gary left the staff room with a glimmer of amusement on his face and went over to a phone on the storeroom wall to try and call for help.

"*Ngor dong sut jar lo.*" A fast speaking voice called in his ear as soon as he lifted the receiver. Gary snarled and put down the receiver and managed not to scream an expletive, as that would have made the jumpy Kylie even jumpier.

While she used the loo, he went into the shop front and switched off all the lights and went to the window and peered outside.

The strange fog was still everywhere and he could only see to the end of the pavement. Gary heard a voice somewhere unseen outside and strained his ears to hear it. He only just caught the cadence of a sentence in a language that was not English.

So he retreated back to the store area and shut the door behind him, just as Kylie remerged from the staff rest room.

"I put the kettle on, do you fancy a tea?" Kylie asked, her coat left behind in the staff room, her cleavage on full bountiful view.

"Yeah, I would." He grinned and followed her back into the staff only area. His mouth was dry and his tongue had a metallic foul taste to it. And, he decided, when the world was falling down around your ears, a cuppa tea couldn't hurt.

"So what's your story then, do you live around here?" Kylie sat cross legged on a mug-ringed table, underneath the painted-over window in the staff room.

"Nah, I got drunk and fell asleep on the last train home and missed my stop." Gary lent against the sink unit next to her and sipped at his refreshing tea.

"God, booze eh? We'd both be alright now if we had stuck to lemonade tonight." Kylie snorted, her nose wrinkling up in an attractive way.

"What do you mean?"

"I don't live in this dump either. I came to see my friend Carly; had a few drinks 'cos my dickhead boyfriend dumped me for some other slag and I fell asleep in the bus shelter and missed all me buses home."

Gary laughed a little, not because of her story, but as an encouragement for her to continue.

"I woke up in frigging fog land, heads back to Carly's and find... find...her..." Kylie trailed off into more heart-wrenching sobs.

Gary put down his tea and moved quickly over to hug her. He clung to her: to comfort her and being scared shitless himself, it made him feel better also.

After a minute her crying subsided and his mind became aware of her large chest pressed against his and the sweet smell of her perfume and he pulled back to see that her red eyes stared into his, her bottom lip trembling. It had been a long time since his wife or any woman had looked at him with the faintest whiff of attraction.

"I ain't thanked you for saving my life tonight," she whispered as he wiped some of the tear lines from her cheeks.

"You're worth saving," he replied, with so much cheese it would cover a whole loaf of toast. Kylie did not seem to notice, or maybe even care.

"After this is all over, I'm gonna jump ya bones big time." Her quivering lip had turned into a lustful one now.

"Well, I won't stop you," Gary replied and their eyes met and they uttered nervous laughs in unison.

Kylie lent forward and kissed the right side of his cheek tenderly; then, daring everything, Gary lent forward and their lips met, going from soft and tender to more ardent kisses in a few seconds.

The window behind Kylie suddenly exploded inwards and two half melted hands reached in to cover her face.

Gary and Kylie screamed in unison as the female Shambler's nails dug into the girl's hair and scalp. Gary grabbed the nearest thing to hand, a blunt bread knife from out of the sink and thrust it up through the Shambler's right eye. He pushed harder and the blade sunk four inches deeper into the creature's head, causing its eyes to pop in an explosion of white and green gore. He grabbed the screaming Kylie around the waist and dragged her off the table into his arms. The Shambler flailed at the knife, then turned its attention back to the retreating Gary and Kylie.

Gary staggered back to the door, pulling Kylie along with him as the creature tried to scramble through the broken window. Gary opened the staff room door, pushed Kylie through and then followed her close behind.

They headed to the front of the shop first, just in time to see one of many Shamblers smash its way through the shop front window, without any regards for the injuries it sustained. More Shamblers crowded behind it and with a wail of terror Gary retreated into the storeroom, pushing Kylie before him now. They raced to the back door without any rational thought, unlocked it and pegged it down the alleyway at the back of the parade of shops.

They hung a left and appeared at another set of shops on the other side. Keeping to the centre of the road, then ran back the way Gary had come, heading for the train station again. Kylie's flapping left hand found his as she used the other to pull down her short skirt.

They both managed to avoid a Shambler that had hidden-in-wait behind a parked car and its melted hand missed them by inches. They ran past the bus shelter and back to the telephone box, before Gary's out-of-shape body hit a brick wall of pain. His left leg cramped up and he had to slow to a fast walking limp. He finally noticed that the fog wasn't as dense as when he had first been here and he could see more of the fields on either side. Kylie screamed and gripped his left arm with both of her long nailed hands, pinching the skin painfully.

Behind them Gary could see dark figures following him from the misty village. Then as they neared the station forecourt their luck ran out. Seven dark figures appeared before him, with odd shaped faces and blocking his escape route.

Gary looked back and saw that ten or more Shamblers were now not far behind him, walking fast in a fanned out U-shape to cut off all routes of escape.

"This ain't fucking fair!" he yelled up to the misty sky, all hope of living past this night now gone.

"What do we do now?" Kylie cried, but Gary wasn't the one to answer her question.

Bright torchlight hit both their faces and a muffled voice shouted: *"Get down on the ground now!"*

It came from the seven figures blocking his way back to the railway station. Gary saw that their faces were not melted but covered in gas masks: all wore black combat uniforms and carried vicious looking guns.

"Get on the ground *now* if you want to live!" one of the soldiers repeated. Gary fell, pulling Kylie down with him to the ground and they hugged the road surface for dear life.

Automatic weapons fire began an instant later and tracers lit up the night. One-by-one the heads of the advancing Shamblers were blown off their shoulders, sending brains everywhere. When their heads exploded, small puffs of green gas billowed from their necks for an instant, like escaping souls.

MOD ESTABLISHMENT
BOSCOMBE DOWN: SUBLEVEL FIVE:
18 MONTHS LATER.

"So why am I here and not some civilian contractor? It's only a broken air conditioning fan for pity's sake." Captain Rutherford of the Royal Engineers grumbled, as he and Doctor Chambers walked through a security door, guarded by two burly Royal Marines.

"Because this is above Top Secret, Captain, and we cannot afford for certain things held here to reach the ears of the general public or the press." The doctor explained as they walked down a corridor with different coloured cables running the length of the walls, near where they met the ceiling

They came to a metal air tight door where Doctor Chambers put his palm onto a hand recognition security scanner, while typing in a seven digit code on the keyboard above.

The door slid sidewards. Captain Rutherford stepped in after the doctor, his toolbox banging into the frame of the door as he entered.

"Please be more careful, this is a sterile airtight secure area." The doctor said sternly and fixed him with an arrogant sneer.

"Understood." The Captain wondered how he got such a bone of a job.

To the left was a glass anti-chamber filled with electrical equipment and monitors of all sorts. In front of it was a room within the room, all soft cream curves and thick glass observation windows. Through the glass of the windows the Captain could see nothing more than some sort of pea soup, thick gaseous fog.

Rutherford stared harder; dark figures could be seen near the glass, but far enough away for the fog to shroud their appearance.

"You have people in there?" Captain Rutherford asked, hating all this cloak and dagger, secret experiments stuff.

"We like to call them survivors, Captain Rutherford, though some of the Techs do call them Shamblers as a little joke." Chambers smiled widely and Rutherford likened it to the smile of a Great White shark.

"Survivors of what?"

"Of the Kendell Wood gas leak tragedy, Captain Rutherford."

Rutherford recalled that a massive gas leak at night had caused the deaths of over fifty villagers in a small rural village a while back. He only really remembered it because an old Sandhurst friend Captain Tom Farrar had died, overcome by gas fumes while trying to evacuate the villagers. Over three hundred people had been saved by the army that night.

"There was no gas leak, was there?" Rutherford was a smart solider and not a stranger to government cover-ups in the past.

"No. A military convoy carrying an old nerve gas from the Second World War was being relocated from a site due for closure. The second vehicle blew a tyre and crashed, spilling its load and one of the unbreakable containers…simply broke." Doctor

Chambers led the Captain past the sealed inner room, towards a ventilation fan set in the wall.

"What happened?"

"Meeting a localised fog bank from the nearby river caused the gas to synthesize with the weather condition and a prevailing wind blew it towards the village. We managed to evacuate most of the villagers, before the fog overran our own men."

"What happened to the ones that came in contact with the fog?" Rutherford asked, as he reached the non-functioning fan.

"Something unprecedented." Chambers explained, dispassionate, as though he was giving a lecture on botany, rather than discussing the deaths of innocent civilians. "The nerve gas had changed over its sixty years in storage and it also changed the people it came in contact with. It did not kill them, but dissolved certain parts of the brain and epidermis. Even the skulls of the victims were weakened for some reason, yet the endoskeleton remained intact; most puzzling."

"This the faulty fan, then?" The Royal Engineer pointed and the doctor nodded in reply.

"Yet the most remarkable thing about the survivors - apart from a regression into more primitive violent state was the loss of motor functions pertaining to their mother tongues." The doctor babbled on, glad to be able to bore another human being with his top secret project.

"And that means?" Captain Rutherford asked the doctor as he unscrewed the bolts to the fan cover.

"All of the villagers and soldiers exposed lost the use of English as their primary language. Men, women and children suddenly began to converse in languages that they could not possibly have learnt. One of the Shamblers speaks Ancient Greek, while another, a lost Babylonian dialect; while others only now speak in German or Spanish. Very much like the effects of the rare Foreign Language Syndrome." The doctor was becoming more excited as he spoke.

"So can you cure them?"

"Once altered by the gas, the process is irreversible. Yet three people exposed to the gas did survive without being altered."

"How?"

"At first we were baffled, and then found out all three had been drinking heavily that night and had high levels of alcohol in their bloodstreams, which rendered them immune to the fog."

"Doctor Chambers to security desk please," came a female voice over an internal intercom system.

"Where are the fan controls?" Rutherford asked, as the doctor made to leave.

"In the control area, there." Chambers pointed to the anti-chamber with monitors they had passed. "Please excuse me for a while."

"Take all the time you like," Rutherford muttered as the doctor left him alone in the large room.

The Royal Engineer soon found out that a wire had come loose on the fan motor and he quickly soldered it back on. Rutherford walked past the eerie soundproof fogbound inner room and headed for the monitor room to test the fan.

The Captain lent on the monitor desk and switched on the fan controls on the wall beside it. He turned to see if it had begun to rotate and accidently dropped the screwdriver in his hand onto the controls, turning the internal speakers on.

A rush of different voices in many different languages invaded the quiet control room.

"Dammit." Rutherford cursed and picked up the screwdriver and was about to switch off the noise, when he spotted a figure on a monitor in the secure room in front of him.

The grotesque melted face seemed familiar and alien at the same time, but the uniform the Shambler wore was that of an infantry officer.

"Tom, Tom Farrar is that you?" Rutherford spoke into a microphone that stuck up from the control desk.

The thing that had been Captain Tom Farrar replied in German. Rutherford replied back in the same language, having been stationed out there for three years and the tale Tom Farrar told was very different to the official version of events.

"Emergency containment procedure red. The door to housing unit five has been breached." The voice echoed through the corridors of sublevel five as Chambers and two of his technicians ran back to the secure area that housed one group of the survivors.

The doorway to the room beyond was on automatic lockdown and was secured from being opened from both inside and out.

Yet through an unseen dent caused by Captain Rutherford's toolbox, a green gas seeped unnoticed out of the secure chamber into the corridor beyond.

Inside the chamber a tall Shambler stuck his head into the spinning ventilation fan that diced his head and brains to mincemeat in seconds. From his neck issued a long stream of green gas that flowed up into the ventilation shaft.

At the door Captain Rutherford's melted hands crashed against the exit, as nine other figures joined him from the open inner housing unit five.

Gary Harrison left his twenty year old girlfriend in the shower and turned on the television in the bedroom of his vast New Zealand home, paid for by a million pounds in British Government hush-money. He towelled his back as the main evening news came on and he watched with horrified interest.

"All flights in and out of England have been cancelled as the green fog that causes violent mental deteriorations in its victims stretches from the south-coast of the country up to the Midlands with no signs of decreasing. The Prime Minister of New Zealand has urged all Commonwealth countries and the United States to take in refugees airlifted from unaffected areas of England, Scotland and Ireland."

Gary got up, went down stairs and turned on the large wall television in his living room. Then went to his bar and selected a bottle of vodka and began to drink.

When Kylie found him, he only had his towel wrapped round his waist and a half-empty bottle of vodka held by the neck in his hands.

"What's the matter, Gary?"

"I think you better have a drink, love." Gary thrust the vodka bottle into her hands, as the news blared on relentlessly before them.

Hersham Horror Books

Fogbound From 5, Alt-Dead, Alt-Zombie all
© Hersham Horror Books

End of the Line © Peter Mark May 2011

Quiet Coach © Alison Littlewood 2011

Fal Vale Junction © Neil Williams 2011

Last Train Home © Mark West 2011

Kriegsmaterial © Adrian Chamberlin 2011

Biographies

Name: Alison Littlewood
Author Website: www.alisonlittlewood.co.uk
Last Publication: *About the Dark*, a short story, appeared in Black Static magazine issue 25 (edited by Andy Cox).
Next Publication: Alison's first novel, *A Cold Season*, will be out in 2012 from Jo Fletcher Books, an imprint of Quercus.
Favourite Horror Writer: It has to be the King...

Name: Neil Williams
Author Website: imaginarydoor.blogspot.com
Last Publication:
My short story *Closer Than You Think in* Ill At Ease from PenMan Press
Next Publication: *The Derelict* a novella from Pendragon Press
Favourite Horror Writer:
M R James

Name: Mark West
Author Website: www.markwest.org.uk
Last Publication: eBook version of *The Mill* from Greyhart Press
Next Publication: *The Lost Film* and *Drive*, two novellas from Pendragon Press
Favourite Horror Writer: Can I choose a few? Stephen King, for opening the field, Robert McCammon for making me cry with *Boy's Life*, Dennis Etchison for his genius and Clive Barker, for *Books Of Blood* and showing me that horror could take place in a world I knew.

Name: Adrian Chamberlin
Author Website: www.archivesofpain.com
Last Publication: *The Caretakers*" (novel) and *Aqua Mortis* (short story in Dark Continents Publishing's Phobophobia anthology).
Next Publication: *War Without An Enemy, Enemy Without A War* in War of the Words Press's "Weird War" anthology.
Favourite Horror Writer: Too close to call between Graham Masterton, F Paul Wilson, Clive Barker and Steve Harris.

Name: Peter Mark May
Author Website: http://www.freewebs.com/darkside6869/index.htm
Last Publication: *Alt-Dead* as Editor & *Dark Waters* a Novella from Damnation Books & *Into The Endless Sea of Night*, short story in the BFS's Full Fathom Forty Anthology.
Next Publication: *Hedge End*: trade paperback from Samhain Publishing USA in 2012
Favourite Horror Writer: M R James, he is the master and F.Paul Wilson, Brian Lumley & H. P. Lovecraft.

Hersham Horror Books

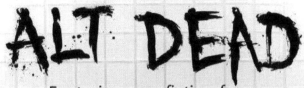

Featuring new fiction from:

Steven Savile & Steve Lockley, Ian Woodhead, Mark West, Dave Jeffery, Stuart Neild, Stephen Bacon, R. J. Gaulding, Zach Black, Katherine Tomlinson, Adrian Chamberlin, Jan Edwards, Stuart Hughes, Richard Farren Barber, Gary McMahon, Stuart Young, Johnny Mains

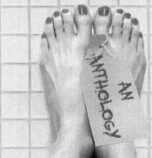

AVAILABLE NOW!

Edited by Peter Mark May

For more information, visit
http://hershamhorrorbooks.webs.com/

Coming Spring/Summer 2012 from
Hersham Horror Books

ALT-ZOMBIE

The Alternative–Zombie anthology containing even more original short stories from authors you love to read. Including stories from writers like Joe McKinney, Gary McMahon, Shaun Jeffrey, Stephen Bacon, Dave Jeffery, Mark West, Willie Meikle, Jan Edwards, David Williamson, Alison Littlewood *and* many, many more....

HTTP://HERSHAMHORRORBOOKS.WEBS.COM/

A big thank you to Ade, Ali, Mark & Neil for all their help in getting FF5 published.

PMM
HHB

Made in the USA
Charleston, SC
19 December 2011